THE

NOTTING HILL MYSTERY

CHARLES WARREN ADAMS

(written under the pseudonym Charles Felix)

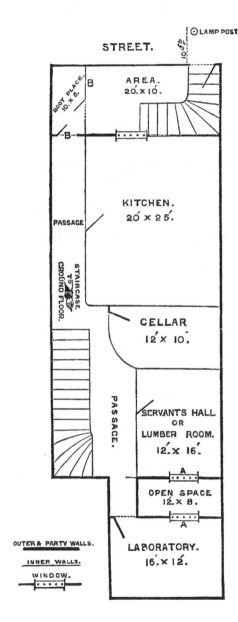

STREET.

⊙ LAMP POST

10 f.b

BOOT PLACE.
10' x 8'

B

AREA.
20' x 10'.

B

PASSAGE

KITCHEN.
20' x 25'.

STAIRCASE
TO
GROUND FLOOR.

CELLAR
12' x 10'.

PASSAGE.

SERVANTS HALL
OR
LUMBER ROOM.
12' x 16'.

A

A

OPEN SPACE
12' x 8'.

A

A

OUTER & PARTY WALLS.

INNER WALLS.

WINDOW.

LABORATORY.
16' x 12'.

BASEMENT FLOOR OF BARON R**'S HOUSE IN RUSSELL PLACE.

Vide Section vii. 8.

THE

NOTTING HILL MYSTERY.

COMPILED BY

CHARLES FELIX

AUTHOR OF 'VELVET LAWN'
ETC.

FROM THE PAPERS OF THE LATE R. HENDERSON, ESQ.

LONDON:

SAUNDERS, OTLEY, AND CO.
66 BROOK STREET, W.

1865.

This edition published in 2012 by

The British Library
96 Euston Road
London NWI 2DB

Cataloguing in Publication Data
A catalogue record for this book is available from The British Library

ISBN 978 0 7123 5859 0

Printed in Great Britain by the MPG Books Group

CONTENTS.

—◆—

CONTENTS.

CONTENTS.

SEEKING THE EVIDENCE

Mike Ashley

According to the late, great aficionado of crime fiction, Julian Symons, writing in 1972, there is 'no doubt' that *The Notting Hill Mystery* is 'the first detective novel'. Any such absolute statement is bound to be challenged, and there are certainly other contenders so it is worth exploring the book's position in the evolution of the detective story in order to understand its significance.

First we need to fix a date. A quick check of the title page of this book states that it was published by Saunders, Otley & Co., in London in 1865, but we can go back further. It was first published as a serial, with no author credit, in *Once a Week*, from 29 November 1862 to 17 January 1863. That serial was illustrated by George Du Maurier (1834–1896), the author of *Trilby* (1894) and grandfather of author Daphne Du Maurier, and his illustrations are reprinted here for the first time.

The 1860s was a period of awakening for the detective novel. The best known of all the early works, *The Moonstone* by Wilkie Collins (1824–1889) was published in 1868 after it had been serialised in *All the Year Round* from January to August of that year. It features Sergeant Cuff who is brought in to find a stolen sacred Indian diamond. He is solid, reliable and thorough, a man of morals, who not only solves the case through methodical investigation, but ensures that the diamond is restored to its rightful home. By the time of *The Moonstone* the detective novel had become established, but what were its antecedents?

Collins's novel appeared at least five years after *The Notting Hill Mystery* and plenty of other books and stories featuring detectives had appeared by then. Perhaps the best known is *Bleak House* by Charles Dickens (1812–1870) originally issued in monthly parts between March 1852 and September 1853. This introduces us to Inspector Bucket 'of the Detective', a wonderfully portrayed character who glides through the pages of the novel just like he slips through the dark and dangerous world of Victorian London, enquiring of the underworld, observing, thinking before he acts, and in every way a true detective. He was modelled to a large degree on a real police detective, Inspector Field. Yet, despite Bucket's noticeable presence in *Bleak House*, his investigations into the death of Mr Tulkinghorn revolve around one of Dickens's many subplots and are not central to the book. One could not describe *Bleak House* as a detective novel, even though it is very evidently a novel featuring a detective.

There had been plenty of short stories involving investigations into crimes, such as 'Das Fräulein von Scuderi' (1819) by E.T.A. Hoffmann (1776–1822), which involves the eponymous lady investigating the innocence of a man arrested for murder. The Fräulein does not solve the crime herself though her pursuit of the truth does lead to the revelation, so she may be seen as an ancestor of the female detective.

The first true literary detective, as we would recognize him, is C. Auguste Dupin, created by Edgar Allan Poe (1809–1849), who appears in three short stories, starting with "The Murders in the Rue Morgue" (1841). Dupin is quite rightly regarded as the true ancestor of Sherlock Holmes, and though he does not earn his living from detection, Dupin is recognised as an expert by the Prefect of Police in Paris and his advice is sought whenever there is an unusual or particularly baffling crime. Poe can justifiably be credited with creating the first modern independent detective, but he did not write a detective novel.

The fact that Poe set his stories in France is because France had become closely associated with the idea of a private detective ever since the days of Eugène François Vidocq (1775–1857), a one-time thief who turned gamekeeper and set up the first plain-clothed investigative unit, the Brigade de la Sûreté, in 1811. The story of his life and the establishment of the Brigade was told in *Mémoires de Vidocq*, published in four volumes during 1828–29. This book, which no doubt embellished the truth with vigorous literary licence was a huge influence on early crime fiction. It was translated into English almost before the ink was dry. An industry erupted, in the English penny dreadfuls, the French sensational literature and the American story papers, of retelling stories (mostly fabricated) from police sources.

Its influence can be seen in the many 'casebook' reminiscences that appeared in subsequent years. One of the earliest was by a forgotten British writer, William Russell (1807–1877), who produced a series of stories for *Chambers's Edinburgh Journal* under the alias 'Waters', purporting to be first-person accounts of a London detective. These first made it into book-form in America as *The Recollections of a Policeman* in 1852 and in Britain as *Recollections of a Detective Police-Officer* in 1856. These were immensely popular, especially in America, where the image of the private detective was further enhanced by the media-hype around the first private detective agency established by Allan Pinkerton (1819–1884) in 1850. Russell wrote many similar books, under various aliases, all in the *faux* autobiographical style of Vidocquian reminiscences, and inspired many imitators.

Amongst them are *The Female Detective* by Andrew Forrester, Jr, and *Revelations of a Lady Detective*, published anonymously but attributed to either Bracebridge Hemyng (1841–1901) or William Stephens Hayward (1835–1870). Both were published in 1864. *The Female Detective* features Mrs Gladden, usually known simply as 'G', who is a genuine consulting detective. Mrs Paschal of *Revelations of a Lady Detective*, on the other hand, is employed by the London Police Force in order to undertake undercover work. Between them they put the female detective firmly on the literary map.

Another nominee for the first female detective is Ruth Trail in *Ruth the Betrayer; or, The Female Spy*, by Edward Ellis, a penny dreadful which appeared in 52 weekly parts starting on 8 February 1862. Ruth isn't really a detective. She's an undercover agent who works on both sides of the law and, as the story develops, is more villain than heroine.

These and similar books such as Mary E. Braddon's *Three Times Dead; or, The Secret of the Heath* (1860), also known as *The Trail of the Serpent*, are works which involve crimes and include some detection, but are in no way detective novels. But they do show a rapidly growing interest by the public in the work of the police, primarily for the more sensational and gruesome activities.

Many believe that the true father of the detective novel was the French writer Émile Gaboriau (1832–1873). Directly in the tradition of Vidocq, but further influenced by Poe, Gaboriau created the police detective Monsieur Lecoq in a series of five novels. In the first, *L'Affaire Lerouge*, he takes a back seat to the retired pawnbroker and consulting detective Father Tabaret, whose deductive skills Lecoq learns and adopts, but in the later novels Lecoq takes centre stage. *L'Affaire Lerouge* was first serialized in the daily newspaper *Le Pays* during 1863, after the magazine appearance of *The Notting Hill Mystery*, but our dates are closing in.

Before he became a full-time novelist, Gaboriau served as secretary to the author Paul Féval (1816–1875) a popular writer of crime thrillers and historical novels who developed a long series of linked novels involving international crime syndicates and conspiracies. Of special interest is *Jean Diable*, published in book-form in France in 1863 though not translated into English till 2004. It was serialized in *Le Siècle* from 1 August to 20 November 1862, concluding just a week before *The Notting Hill Mystery* began. Set in 1816, *Jean Diable* features the Scotland Yard detective Gregory Temple (even though Scotland Yard was not established until 1829). Temple has a painstaking, methodical and analytical approach to detection. The serial, long and rambling like most newspaper *feuilleton*'s of the day, involves Temple's attempts to convict a master criminal. To French readers, the master criminal was more the hero than the English detective and in the final episode Jean Diable eludes conviction even though Temple has at last found the one vital clue that proves his guilt. The novel is undoubtedly crime fiction and is a step forward from the casebook-style novels, focusing on the tussle between a police detective and a master criminal. It is arguably the first police-procedural novel, and is certainly the closest to a genuine detective novel yet published.

So what makes *The Notting Hill Mystery* different? – and it is, quite startlingly different. For a start the investigation is by an insurance agent, Ralph Henderson. The novel is his report, presenting all the evidence to prove, to his satisfaction, that Madame R** was murdered and how. His report includes statements from a host of witnesses, including police statements, all of which are meticulously analysed and methodically assessed. There are no sensational chases, no battles with criminals, no undercover work. In that sense the novel is remarkably modern in its presentation. It seems to grow in entirely new soil, with no relationship to previous casebook reminiscences.

There are precedents, but only short stories. Wilkie Collins had written 'Who is the Thief?' (*Atlantic Monthly*, April 1858), later incorporated into his novel *The Queen of Hearts* (1859) as 'The Biter Bit'. It's a fairly light-hearted story, telling, by a series of extracts from police memoranda, how the villain was identified. In 'Hunted Down' (*New York Ledger*, 20 August–3 September 1859), Charles Dickens tells of a girl whose life is insured and who then mysteriously dies. Mr. Meltham, an employee of the insurance company, investigates her death and identifies the perpetrator.

The author of *The Notting Hill Mystery* would have almost certainly read those stories and used both ideas and techniques in his serial, taking them to an extreme never seen before, and rarely seen since. In that sense the book is unique and is, so far as the record shows, the first full-length modern English-language detective novel.

Which leaves us with the mystery of the authorship. When the story was serialised in *Once a Week* there was no author credit, but when published as a book in 1865 it bore the by-line Charles Felix. Felix had written at least one earlier crime novel, *Velvet Lawns*, published by the same firm, Saunders, Otley & Co., in 1864. Various names have been suggested as to his true identity, but it wasn't until early 2011 that the American collector and bibliophile Paul Collins, writing in the *New York Times* Sunday Book Review, drawing upon contemporary evidence, revealed that Felix was Charles Warren Adams (1833–1903), the sole proprietor of Saunders, Otley.

The original Messrs Saunders and Otley had died a few years earlier, and Adams was unable to salvage the firm and return it to its glory days of the 1830s when it had published the likes of Edward Bulwer (later Bulwer-Lytton) and Captain Frederick Marryat. The firm went into liquidation in 1869. Adams became the Secretary of the Anti-Vivisection Society and it was in this capacity that his one hitherto claim to fame, or notoriety, arose. Also on the Society's committee was Mildred Coleridge, great-grand niece of the poet Samuel Taylor Coleridge. In November 1883 she turned her back on her family and moved in with Adams, much to the embarrassment of her father, the first Baron Coleridge who was also the Chief Justice. Her eldest brother, Bernard, wrote her a letter saying what a scoundrel he thought Adams was. This led to a major libel case in the Queen's Bench Division which dragged on for over two years to no one's complete satisfaction. In the interim, Adams and Mildred Coleridge married in June 1885 and remained together until Adams died in July 1903.

Mildred lived on until January 1929. Did she, I wonder, know that he was the author of the first modern English detective novel?

NOTTING HILL MYSTERY.

———◆———

Mr. R. Henderson to the Secretary of the
——— Life Assurance Association.

'Private Enquiry Office, Clement's Inn,
'17th Jan., 1858.

'GENTLEMEN,

'In laying before you the extraordinary revelations arising from my examination into the case of the late Madame R**, I have to apologise for the delay in carrying out your instructions of November last. It has been occasioned, not by any neglect on my part, but by the unexpected extent and intricacy of the enquiry into which I have been led. I confess that after this minute and laborious investigation I could still

B

have wished a more satisfactory result, but a perusal of the accompanying documents, on the accuracy and completeness of which you may fully rely, will I doubt not satisfy you of the unusual difficulty of the case.

' My enquiries have had reference to a policy of assurance for 5000*l*., the maximum amount permitted by your rules, on the life of the late Madame R**, effected in your office by her husband, the Baron R**, and bearing date 1st November, 1855. Similar policies were held in the —— of Manchester, the —— of Liverpool, the —— of Edinburgh, and the —— of Dublin, the whole amounting to 25,000*l*.; the dates, 23rd December, 1855, 10th January, 25th January, and 15th February, 1856, respectively, being in effect almost identical. These companies joined in the instructions under which I have been acting; and, from the voluminous nature of this letter and its enclosures, I shall be obliged by your considering my present reply as addressed to them conjointly with yourselves.

' Before entering upon the subject of my

investigations, it may be as well to recapi-
tulate the circumstances under which they
were originated. Of these the first was
the coincidence of dates, above noticed; and
an apparent desire on the part of the assurer
to conceal from each of the various offices'
the fact of similar policies having been
elsewhere simultaneously effected. On examining further into the matter your Board
was also struck with the peculiar conditions
under which Madame R**'s marriage appeared to have taken place, and the relation
in which she had formerly stood to the
Baron. To these points, therefore, my
attention was especially directed, and the
facts thus elicited form a very important
link in the singular chain of evidence I have
been enabled to put together.

'The chief element of suspicion, however, was to be found in the very unusual
circumstances attendant on the death
of Madame R**, especially following so
speedily as it did on the assurance for so
large an aggregate amount. This lady
died suddenly on the 15th March, 1857,

from the effects of a powerful acid taken, it is supposed, in her sleep, from her husband's laboratory. In the Baron's answers to the usual preliminary enquiries, forwarded for my assistance, and herewith returned, there is no admission of any propensity to somnambulism. Shortly, however, after the occurrence had been noticed in the public prints, a letter to the Secretary of the Association from a gentleman recently lodging in the same house with Baron R**, gave reason to suspect that in this respect, at least, some concealment had been practised, and the matter was then placed in my hands.

'On receipt of your instructions, I at once put myself in communication with Mr. Aldridge, the writer of the letter in question. That gentleman's evidence certainly goes to show that, within at least a very few months after the date of the latest policy, Baron R** was not only himself aware of such a propensity in his wife, but desirous of concealing it from others. Mr. Aldridge's statements are also to a certain extent supported by those of two other witnesses; but, unfortunately, there are, as will be seen, circumstances calculated to throw considerable doubt upon the whole of this evidence, and especially on that of Mr. Aldridge, from which alone the more important part of the inference is drawn. The same must, unfortunately, be said with regard to some other parts of the evidence, as will be more clearly seen when the case itself is before you.

' From his statement, however, in conjunction with other circumstances, I learned enough to induce me to extend my researches to another very singular case, which not long since had given rise to considerable comment.

' You will, no doubt, remember that in the autumn of 1856 a gentleman of the name of Anderton was arrested on suspicion of having poisoned his wife, and that he committed suicide whilst awaiting the issue of a chemical enquiry into the cause of her death. This enquiry resulted in an acquittal, no traces of the suspected poison being

found; and the affair was hushed up as
speedily as possible, many of Mr. Anderton's
connections being of high standing in society,
and naturally anxious for the honour of
the family. I must, however, acknowledge
the readiness with which, in the interest
of justice, I have been furnished by them
with every facility for pushing my enquiries, the results of which are now before
you.

'In reviewing the whole facts, and more
especially the series of remarkable coincidences of dates, &c., to which I beg to
direct your most particular attention, two
alternatives present themselves. In the
first we must altogether ignore a chain of
circumstantial evidence so complete and
close-fitting in every respect, as it seems
almost impossible to disregard; in the
second, we are inevitably led to a conclusion so at variance with all the most
firmly established laws of nature, as it seems
almost equally impossible to accept. The
one leaves us precisely at the point from
which we started; the other involves the

imputation of a series of most horrible and complicated crimes.

'Between these alternatives I am constrained to confess my own inability, after long and careful study, to decide. I have determined, therefore, simply to submit for your consideration the facts of the case as they appear in the depositions of the several parties from whom my information has been obtained. These I have arranged, as far as possible, in the form in which they would be laid before counsel, should it ultimately be deemed advisable to bring the affair into Court. In view, however, of the extreme length of the case, I have given, in a condensed form, the substance of such of the depositions as did not seem likely to suffer from such treatment. The more important I have left to tell their own tale, and, in any case, my abstract may be at once checked by the originals, all of which are enclosed.

'Should your conclusions be such as have been forced upon myself, further deliberation will yet be required with reference to the course to be pursued; a point on which, in such case, I confess myself almost equally unable to advise.   Whether, in a matter so surrounded with suspicion, it might not be well, in any event, to resist the claim, is certainly a question to be considered.   On the other hand, even assuming the fullest proof of the terrible crimes involved, it is a matter calling for no less careful considera- tion, whether they would be found of a nature to bring the criminal within reach of the law.   For the present, however, our concern is with the facts of the case, and ulterior questions had better be left on one side until that issue is decided, when I shall, no doubt, hear further from you on the subject.

' In conclusion, I must trouble you with a few words on a point which seems to re- quire explanation.   I allude to the apparent prominence I have been compelled to afford to the workings of what is called "Mesmeric Agency."   Those, indeed, who are so un- fortunate as to be the victims of this delusion, would doubtless find in it a simple, though terrible solution of the mystery we are endeavouring to solve. But while frankly admitting that it was the passage from the *Zoïst* Magazine, quoted in the course of the evidence, which first suggested to my mind the only conclusion I have as yet been able to imagine, I beg at the outset most distinctly to state, that I would rather admit my own researches to have been baffled by an illusory coincidence, than lay myself open to the imputation of giving the slightest credit to that impudent imposture. We must not, however, forget that those whose lives have been passed in the deception of others, not unfrequently end by deceiving themselves. There is, therefore, nothing incredible in the idea that the Baron R** may have given sufficient credence to the statement of the *Zoïst* above-mentioned, for the suggestion to his own mind of a design, which by the working of a true, though most mysterious, law of Nature, may really have been carried

out.   Such, at least, is the only theory by
which I can attempt, in any way, to elucidate this otherwise unfathomable mystery.

'Awaiting the honour of your further
commands,

'I am,
Gentlemen,
Very faithfully yours,
'RALPH HENDERSON.'

THE CASE.

Extracts from Correspondence of the Honourable Catherine B**.*

1. *From Lady Boleton to Honourable C. B** (undated), about October or November of* 1832.

' Oh, auntie, auntie, what shall I do? For three nights I have not closed my eyes, and I would not write even to you, auntie dear, because I kept hoping that, after all, things might come right, and he would come back again. Oh, how I have listened to every sound, and watched the road till my poor eyes ache! And now this is the fourth day since he went away, and, oh, auntie, I am so frightened, for I am sure he is gone after

---

* Great-aunt of the late Mrs. Anderton. The object of going so far back will presently appear.

that dreadful man, and, oh, if he should
meet him, I know something terrible will
happen, for you can't tell how he looked,
poor Edward, I mean, when he went away.
But, indeed, auntie, you must not be angry
with him, for I know it was all my own
fault, for I ought to have told him everything long ago, though indeed, indeed, I
never cared for him, and I do love dear
Edward so dearly.   I was afraid. . . . . .

[Here the MS. becomes in places very
blotted and illegible.]

. . . and I thought it was at an end, and
then . . . . . and only a fortnight ago we
were so happy . . . . married hardly seven
months and . . . . but you must not
think I am complaining of him, dear auntie,
for you don't know how . . . . Only
if you can, come to me, for I feel getting so
ill, and you know it is only . . . . . God
bless you, auntie; oh, do come to me if you
can.

'GERTRUDE BOLETON.'

2. *Extract of letter from the Same to the Same, written about four days later.*

*   *   *   *   *

' I am sorry to hear you are so ill; don't try to come, darling auntie; I shall do some-how, and if not, anything is better than this horrible suspense . . . . . No tidings yet, but I cannot write more, for I can hardly see to guide the pen, and my poor head seems to open and shut. God bless you, auntie.   ' G.'

' I open my letter to thank you so much for sending dear kind Mrs. Ward; she came in so unexpectedly [in a blue *] just as if she had come from heaven. I wonder if she has seen Ed. . . .'

[Here the MS. ends suddenly.]

3. *From Mrs. Ward to Honourable C. B**, enclosing the above.*

' Beechwood,† Tuesday night.

' MY DEAR CATHERINE,

' I fear I have but a poor account to give you of our dear Gertrude.   Poor child!

* Scratched out.
† The residence of Sir Edward Boleton.

when I came into the room, and saw her looking so pale and wan, and with great black circles round her eyes, I could scarcely keep in my own tears. She gave a little cry of joy when she saw me, and threw herself upon my neck; but a moment after, turned to the writing table and tore open the letter I send you with this, and which was lying ready for the post. The long-continued strain seems to have been too much for her, and she had hardly written a line when her head began to wander, as you will see from the conclusion of her postscript, and in trying to write her husband's name she broke down altogether, and went off into a fit of hysterics which lasted for several hours. She is now, I am thankful to say, comparatively calm again, though at times her head still wanders, and she seems quite unable to close her eyes, but lies in her bed looking straight before her, and occasionally talking to herself in a low voice, but without seeming to notice anything. I have endeavoured, as far as I dared, to draw from her

the history of this sad affair, but can get
nothing, poor child, but eager assurances
that it was 'all her fault,' and that 'indeed,
indeed, *he* was not to blame.'   It seems as
though my coming—though certainly a
great relief to her—had had the effect of
putting her on her guard lest anything
should escape her unfavourable to her husband, and her whole faculties seem to be
concentrated in the endeavour to shield him
from reproach.   I fear, however, there can
be no doubt that he has been very seriously
to blame; indeed, from all I can gather,
the fault seems to have been entirely on
his side.   What is the precise history of
this unhappy business I have not been able
to learn; but it seems that Sir Edward,
who is certainly a most violent young
man, and I fear also of a most jealous temperament, contracted some suspicion with
regard to that Mr. Hawker who so perseveringly persecuted poor Gertrude the winter
before last, and to have left Beechwood,
after a very distressing scene, in pursuit of
him.   Mr. Hawker is supposed to be on

the Continent, and it is known that Sir
Edward took the Dover Road, which, as
you know, passes close by this place. This
is all I can at present learn with any certainty, though I hear but too much from the
servants, who are all in such a state of
indignation at Sir Edward's treatment of
their mistress, that I have the utmost difficulty in restraining it from finding some
open vent. Should I hear more, I will of
course let you know at once; but mean-
while I cannot conceal from you my deep
anxiety for our dear Gertrude, whose poor
little heart seems quite broken, and for
whom I am in hourly dread of the effect
but too likely to be produced, in her present delicate state, by the anxiety and ter-
ror from which she is suffering . . . . You
know how much I always disliked the
match, and I feel more than ever the
impropriety of consigning so young and
sensitive a girl to the care of a man
of such notoriously uncontrollable temper.
Poor thing! this is evidently not the first
time she has suffered from it, and even
should she herself escape without injury

to her constitution, I dread the effect upon the child . . . . . And now I must close this long and sad letter, but will write again should anything fresh occur; meantime, I cannot be longer away just now from Gertrude's side. I hope your own health is improving. My love to little Henry, and tell him to be very good while I am away.

'Your affectionate

'HELEN WARD.'

4. *The Same to the Same.*

'Beechwood, Monday morning.

'MY DEAR CATHERINE,

'I am sorry to say I can still send you no better account of poor Gertrude. Since I last wrote by Saturday evening's post,* very little change has taken place, though she is certainly more restless, poor child, and I fear also, if anything, weaker. She now constantly asks for letters, and seems impressed with the idea that we are keeping them from her, as indeed, in her present

* The letter is omitted as containing nothing of any importance.

C

state, I should, I think, take the respon-
sibility of doing, if any arrived. The newspaper I have always kept from her until
it has first been carefully examined. I am
dreading fever, though by the doctor's
advice I have not attempted to dissuade
her from getting up. The exertion, however, is almost more than she can bear, and
I am looking anxiously for his next visit.
She lies all day on the sofa, looking out of
the window, which commands a view of
the Dover Road.   This morning she seems
growing more and more restless, and I am
waiting with inexpressible anxiety for Dr.
Travers.

' Eleven o'clock.

' The doctor has been, and confirms my
fear of approaching fever, which, however,
he says may possibly pass off.   He has
ordered me to lie down at once for some
hours, as I have hardly been in bed since I
arrived, and he says if fever should come
on I shall want all the strength I can get.
I shall keep this letter open, to send you by
the evening's post the latest account.

'Wednesday.

'All is over. I can hardly command
myself sufficiently to write, and yet I must
tell you what has happened. Oh, my dear Catherine, how shall I ever forgive myself for
leaving poor dear Gertrude; and yet I know
that this is foolish, for I was ordered to do
so for her sake.   But I must come at once
to the sad news I have to tell.   I left poor
Gertrude in the charge of her maid, with
strict injunctions to call me if there should
be any change; but the poor child seems
suddenly to have grown quieter, and at
length to have fallen asleep.   The maid
watched her until just four o'clock, when,
overcome with weariness, she herself dropped
off into a doze, and on waking at a little
before five, was horrified to find herself
alone.   She flew at once to me, but I had
hardly got to the top of the stairs when
some one came running up to say that the
postman was below, and had just met with
poor Gertrude, who had been watching for
him at the gate.   She enquired eagerly
after letters, and on being told there were

c 2

none, asked for the newspaper, which she
at once hurried away with into a part of
the grounds called the Wilderness, while
the postman, fearing from her manner that
something was amiss, came on to the house
to tell what had occurred. I need not tell
you with what anxiety I hastened to the
Wilderness, and there, poor girl, we found
her, stretched upon the turf close by the
edge of the lake, with the fatal newspaper
in her hand. I had her taken carefully to
the house, and a man despatched on horse-
back for the doctor; but before he arrived
she had recovered consciousness, only, poor
child, to be at once seized with the signs of
her approaching trouble. From that moment until she breathed her last—an hour
ago—I have never left her side. After
nearly thirty hours of the most terrible
suffering I have ever witnessed, she at
length gave birth to two poor little girls,
both so small and weak-looking that it is
quite piteous to see them. The elder in
especial, which was born about an hour
before the second, is so weak and sickly,

'I hastened to the wilderness, and there, poor girl, we
found her stretched upon the turf close by the edge of
the lake, with the fatal newspaper in her hand.'

that the doctor says it is scarcely possible it can live, and, indeed, one can hardly hope that it may. The second seems stronger, but both are very small and weakly even considering their premature birth.

' Poor Gertrude now sank rapidly, and though every means was tried, and she still lingered on for three or four hours, she at length sank altogether, passing away at the last so quietly that we hardly knew that she was gone. Poor darling, I always loved her as being such a favourite with you all . . . . . . One word before I close as to the paper which was the unhappy cause of this terrible blow. It contained, as I had feared, the long dreaded intelligence of Sir Edward's fatal quarrel with Mr. H.; and I send it off by the same post, as you will wish to know the sad particulars. I cannot write more now, for I am fairly worn out, and must take some rest. You know how deeply I sympathise with you . . . . . .

' Most affectionately yours,

' HELEN WARD.'

5. *Extract from the* 'Morning Herald,' *of the —th of November,* 183—.

'*Fatal Duel at Dieppe.*—We learn from the Paris papers that an extraordinary and fatal duel took place some days since, in the neighbourhood of Dieppe, between two Englishmen, neither of whom have as yet been identified. It appears that the parties encountered each other in the courtyard of the Hotel de l'Europe, where one of them, whose linen bears the mark of " C. G. H.," had been staying for some days. The new comer at once assailed the other evidently with the most opprobrious language, to which Mr. H. replied with equal warmth, but the conversation, being carried on in English, was unfortunately not understood by any one present. The altercation at length grew so warm that the landlord was compelled to interfere, and the parties then left the hotel together. A few hours afterwards Mr. H. returned, and calling for his bill, hastily packed his portmanteau, and departed. He has since been traced to Paris, where he was lost sight of altogether.

Early the next morning a rumour spread that the body of an Englishman had been found in a vineyard, about a mile distant from the town, and on enquiry it proved that the victim was no other than the gentleman with whom the dispute had occurred on the previous night. It was evident on examination that the unfortunate man must have fallen in fair fight, though no seconds appear to have been present during the encounter. A pistol, recently discharged, was firmly grasped in the hand of the dead man; and at a dozen paces distance lay its fellow, evidently the weapon with which he had been killed. The fatal wound, too, was exactly in that portion of the chest which would be exposed to an adversary's fire, and had evidently pierced the heart, so that death must have been instantaneous. The weapons with which the fatal duel was fought appear to have been the property of the deceased. They were a very handsome pair of duelling pistols, hair triggers, and evidently of English make. On the butt of each was a small silver shield, bearing the initials " E. B.," and an armed hand grasping a crossbow. The initials of the unfortunate gentleman's opponent were, as we have said, " C. G. H."; and we have reason to fear that the victim was a young baronet, of considerable landed property, with whose sudden departure for the Continent rumour has for some time been busy.

' Since our first edition went to press, we have received further particulars, which leave no room for doubt that the victim of the above fatal occurrence was, as we feared, Sir Edward Boleton, Bart., of Beechwood, Kent; but the cause of the duel, and the name of his opponent, still remain a mystery. The unfortunate gentleman leaves behind him a young wife, to whom he was united but a few months since. Failing a male heir, the baronetcy will now, we understand, become extinct, while the bulk of the estates will pass to a distant connection. The widow, however, is, we believe, in possession of considerable independent property.'

6. *Mrs. Ward to Honourable C. B**.*

'July, 1836.

' MY DEAR CATHERINE,

*   *   *   *   *   *

' You ask me whether I am satisfied with what I saw the other day of poor Gertrude Boleton's little ones. To say that I am satisfied with their appearance would, poor little things, be hardly true, for they are still anything but healthy — poor Gertie especially looking like a faded lily. The younger, however, is certainly improved, and will, I hope, do well, and I quite think that they both are better where they are than they could possibly be elsewhere. It is indeed sad, poor things, that they should have no near relation with whom they could live, but I quite agree with you that, in your state of health, it would not only be too great an undertaking for yourself, but would be by no means beneficial to them. Indeed I am convinced that on every account they are best where they are. The air of Hastings seems to suit them; and in the higher part of the town, where Mrs.

Taylor lives, is bracing without being too cold. Mrs. Taylor herself is a most excellent person, and extremely fond of them. She seems especially interested in poor Gertie, and never wearies of relating instances of the wonderful sympathy between the twins. This sympathy seems even more physical than mental. According to Mrs. Taylor, every little ailment that affects the one is immediately felt also by the other, though with this difference, that your namesake, Katie, is but very slightly affected by Gertie's troubles, while she, poor child, I suppose from the greater delicacy of her constitution, is rendered seriously ill by every little indisposition of her sister. I have often heard of the strong physical sympathies between twins, but never met myself with so marked an instance. Both, unfortunately, are sadly nervous, though here, too, the elder is the greater sufferer, while in the younger it seems to take the form of extreme quickness of perception. . . . Of course, as they grow up, they should be placed with some one of their own rank of

life, but for the present I think poor Mrs.
Taylor will do very well. . . . I shall
be at Hastings again next month, and will
write when I have seen them.

'Affectionately yours,

'HELEN WARD.'

7. *From Mrs. Taylor to Honourable C. B***.

(About January, 1837.)

'HONNERED MISS,

'with My Humbel duty to Your ladyshipp and i am trewly sory to sai as mis
Gerterud hav took a terrabel bad cold
wich I Was afeard as she wud do has Miss
kattarren av Likewise Had wun for 2 dais
past wich i Am sory to sai as mis gerterud
is wuss than mis Kattaren but Hoping she
wil be Well agen Sone wich has I hev told
your Honnered Ladyshipp they as allers
the same trubbels ony pore mis gerterud
allers hav them Wust. Honnered Miss
the docter have ben her wich he sais has
mis Kattaren his quite wel agen he sais
Honnered mis he hops mis gerterud will

sone be wel 2.   honnered Mis yore Humbel
serv^t. to comand   ' SARAH TAYLER.'

8. *From Same to Same.*

(About June, 1837.)

' HONNERED Mis

'with My humbel Duty to Yore ladyshipp hand i am trewly thenkfull to sai the
dere childern are both quit wel wich miss
Kattaren made erself Hill on teusday and
pore miss gerterud were verry bad in conn-
sekens for 3 dais but his now quit wel
agen.   honnered mis yore Ladyshipps humbel ser^t. to command   ' SARAH TAYLER.'

9. *From Same to Same.*

'July, 1837.

' HONNERED MIS

' with my humbel duty to Yore ladyshipp
hand wud you plese Cum Direcly wich sum-
think Dredfull hav apenned to pore mis
Kattaren honnered mis Yore Ladyshipps
humbel ser^t to comand

' SARAH TAYLER.'

10. *Mr. Ward to Honourable C. B**.*

'Marine Hotel, Hastings,
'July 12, 1837.

'DEAR MISS B**,

'Helen was unfortunately prevented from leaving home at the time your letter arrived, so, as the matter seemed urgent, I thought it best to come myself. I am sorry to have to send you such very unsatisfactory intelligence. Poor little Catherine has been lost —stolen, I am afraid, by gipsies—and I have hitherto been quite unable to find any clue to their whereabouts. It appears that Mrs. Taylor took them for a trip with some friends of hers to Fairlie Down, where they fell in with a gang of gipsies, of whom, however, they did not take any particular notice. They had taken their dinner with them, and after finishing it sat talking for some time, when suddenly the child was missed; and, though they hunted in every direction for several hours, no trace of her could be found. On returning to the place where the gipsies had been seen, the camp was found broken up, and the track, after passing near where they had been sitting, was lost on the hard road. Unfortunately, poor Mrs. Taylor—who seems quite distracted by what has happened—could think of nothing at first but writing to you, and it was only by the gossip of her friends, who live at some distance from the town, that the intelligence at length reached the police. Enquiries were being set on foot when I arrived last night, but I fear that, from the time that has been lost, there is now but little chance of recovering the poor child. I have advertised in all directions, and offered a large reward, but I have little hope of the result, nor are the police more sanguine than myself. Unfortunately poor Catherine's dark, gipsy-like complexion, and black eyes and hair, will render it easy to disguise her features, while her quick intelligence and lithe, active figure, will make her only too valuable an acquisition to the band. I need not tell you how grieved I am at this fresh trouble to these poor children, and I fear Gertrude will suffer severely from the loss of her sister, with whom she has, as you know, so extraordinary a bond of sympathy. I am going now to the police station to consult on further measures, and will write to you again by to-morrow morning's post.

'Ever, dear Miss B**,

'Very truly yours,

'HENRY WARD.'

11. *Mrs. Vansittart to the Honourable C. B**.*

'Grove Hill House Academy, Hampstead Heath,

'Wednesday, May 1, 1842.

'MADAM,

'I have much pleasure in complying with your request for a monthly report of the health and progress of my very interesting young friend and pupil, Miss Boleton. In a moral and educational point of view nothing could possibly be more satisfactory. . . . Of my dear young friend's health I am compelled, however, to lament my inability to address you in the same congratulatory terms which in all other matters I am happily so well authorised to employ. Notwithstanding the extreme salubrity of the atmosphere by which in this justly celebrated locality she is surrounded, and I trust I may venture to add the unremitting attention she has experienced both at my own hands and those of my medical and educational assistants, her general health is still, I regret to say, very far from having attained to that condition of entire convalescence at which I trust she may yet, with the advantage of a prolonged residence upon the Heath, before very long arrive. My medical adviser, Dr. Winstanley,—a physician of European reputation, and one in whom I can repose the most entire confidence,—informs me that Miss Boleton is suffering from no especial ailment, though subject from time to time to fits of illness to which it is often difficult to assign any sufficient cause, and which after a while disappear as strangely as they arose. He trusts with me that the pure air of the Heath, which so far as we can venture to believe has already been beneficial to his interesting patient, will in course of time effect a radical cure.   The loss of her young sister, of which you informed me on her first joining our little society, inflicted, beyond doubt, a very serious blow upon her naturally feeble constitution; but I trust that its effects are already passing away.   I shall, of course, adhere strictly to your instructions never in any way to allude to the sad occurrence in conversation with Miss Boleton, and have thought it advisable not to acquaint her companions with the fact.   On the 1st of next month I shall again do myself the honour of acquainting you with the progress made by my interesting young friend, and have little doubt of being at that time able to furnish you with a satisfactory account of her physical no less than of her moral and intellectual advancement.   For the present, dear madam, permit me to subscribe myself,

' Your very faithful

' And obliged servant,

' AMELIA DOROTHEA VANSITTART.'

' To the Honourable Catherine B**.'

12. *Mrs. Ward to the Honourable C. B***.

'14 June, 1851.

'MY DEAR CATHERINE,

'Very many thanks for your early intelligence of dear Gertrude's engagement. I congratulate you most heartily, though, as you have yourself alluded to it, I cannot deny that I should have been better pleased had Mr. Anderton, in addition to all his other good qualities, possessed that of a somewhat less nervous and excitable temperament. I have always liked him much; but with poor Gertrude's own delicate constitution I cannot but fear the results of such an union upon both.   However, it is impossible to have everything, and in all other respects he seems more than unexceptionable, so once more I congratulate you heartily. Are you really thinking of coming up to the Exhibition ? . . . . Give my best love to dear Gertrude, and say all that is kind and proper for us to her *fiancé*. Ever, dear Catherine,

'Affectionately yours,

'HELEN WARD.'

Section II.

1.—*Memorandum by Mr. Henderson.*

WE now come to that portion of Mrs. Anderton's* history which embraces the period between her marriage and the commencement of her last illness. For this I have been compelled to have recourse to various quarters. The information thus afforded is very complete, and taken in conjunction with what we have already seen in Miss B——'s correspondence of the previous life of this unfortunate lady, throws considerable light upon two important points to be hereafter noticed. The depositions, however, unavoidably run to a greater length than, at this stage of the proceedings, their bearing on the main points of the case would render necessary; and

---

* The late Miss Boleton.

I have therefore condensed them for your use in the following memorandum. Any portion, not sufficiently clear, may be elucidated by a reference to the originals enclosed.

Mr. Anderton was a gentleman of good origin, closely connected with some of the first families in Yorkshire, where he had formed the acquaintance of Miss Boleton, while staying at the house of her great aunt, Miss B——. He appears to have been of a most gentle and amiable disposition, though unfortunately so shy and retiring as to have formed comparatively very few intimacies. All, however, who could be numbered among his acquaintance seem to have been equally astonished at the charge brought against him on the death of his wife, with whom he was always supposed, though from his retired habits little was positively known, to have lived upon terms of the most perfect felicity. As the event proved, the case would in effect never have come on for trial; but, had it done so, the defence would have brought forward overwhelming evidence of the incredibility of such a crime on the part of one of so gentle and affectionate a disposition.

During the four years and a-half of their married life there does not appear to have been a cloud upon their happiness. Mrs. Anderton's letter to her great aunt, Miss B—— (to whom I am indebted for almost the whole of the important information I have been able to collect respecting the family), are full of expressions of attachment to her husband and instances of his devotion to her. Copies of several of these letters are enclosed, and from these it will be seen how unvarying was their attachment to each other. Throughout the entire series, extending over the whole period of her married life, there is not a single expression which could lead to any other conclusion.

It is, however, evident that the delicate health with which Mrs. Anderton had been afflicted from her birth, still continued, and in two instances we have indications of the

same mysterious attacks noticed in the
letter of Mrs. Vansittart before quoted.
These, however, appear to have been but
very slight.   They had for some years been
of more and more rare occurrence, and
from this date (October 1852) we have
no further record of anything of the kind.
Still, Mrs. Anderton's general health continued very unsatisfactory, and almost
everything seems to have been tried by her
for its improvement.   Among the enclosed
correspondence are letters dated from
Baden, Ems, Lucca, Cairo, and other places
to which the Andertons had, at different
times, gone for the health of one or other,
Mr. Anderton being also, as stated in Mrs.
Ward's letter of the 14th June, 1851,* extremely delicate.

Of this gentleman, all accounts agree in
stating that the chief ailment was a constitutional nervousness, mental as well as
physical.   The latter showed itself in the
facility with which, though by no means

* Section I., No. 12.

deficient in courage, he could be startled
by any sudden occurrence, however simple ;
the former, in his extreme sensitiveness to
the opinions of those about him, and his
dread of the slightest shadow of reproach
on the name of which he was so justly
proud. In the accompanying documents
you will find instances of both these idio-
syncrasies.

In the summer of 1854 Mr. Anderton's
attention seems to have been drawn to the
subject of Mesmerism. They had been
spending some weeks at Malvern, where
this science seems particularly in vogue, and
had there made acquaintance with several
of the patients at the different water-cure
establishments, by some of whom Mr. Anderton was strongly urged to have recourse to
mesmeric treatment both for Mrs. Anderton
and himself.

The constant solicitations of these en-
thusiastic friends seem at length to have
produced their effects, and the favourite
operator of the neighbourhood was requested to try his skill on these new

patients. On Mr. Anderton the only result seems to have been the inducing of such a state of irritation as might not unreasonably have been expected from so nervously excitable a temperament, in presence of the 'manipulations' to which the votaries of mesmerism are subjected. In the case of Mrs. Anderton, however, the result was, or was supposed to be, different. Whether from some natural cause that, at the time, escaped attention, or whether solely from that force of imagination from which such surprising results are often found to arise, I cannot of course say; but it is certain that some short time after the mesmeric 'séances' had commenced, a decided though slight improvement was perceptible. This continued until the departure of the operator for Germany, which country he had only recently left on a short visit to England.

Notwithstanding the worse than failure in his own case, the certainly curious coincidence of his wife's recovery seems to have entirely imposed on Mr. Anderton, whose susceptibility of disposition appears indeed to have laid him especially open to the practices of quacks of every kind. So great was now his faith in this new remedy that he actually proposed to accompany the Professor to Germany rather than that his wife should lose the benefit of the accustomed 'manipulations.' He had proceeded to London, for the purpose of making the necessary preparations, when he was induced to pause by the remonstrances of several of his friends, who represented to him that a winter in the severe climate of Dresden—the place to which the Professor was bound—would probably be fatal to one of Mrs. Anderton's delicate constitution.

His medical adviser also, though himself professing belief in mesmerism, gave a similar opinion, while at the same time he obviated the difficulty respecting the mesmeric treatment of Mrs. Anderton, by offering an introduction to 'one of the most powerful mesmerists in Europe,' who had recently arrived in London, and who eventually proved to be the so-styled Baron R**.

This introduction appears to have finally decided Mr. Anderton against the Dresden expedition ; and, after a brief experience of his manipulations, Mrs. Anderton herself seems to have derived, in imagination at least, more benefit from them than even from those of her late attendant. So thoroughly were they both impressed with the beneficial results of the Baron's 'passes,' &c., that Mr. Anderton, who had now re-solved to settle in London for the autumn and winter, went so far as to take a ready-furnished house at Notting Hill, for the express purpose of having his new professor in his immediate neighbourhood. Here the 'séances' were continued often twice or three times a-day, and though, of course, no one in his senses could really attribute such a result to the exercises of the Baron, it is certain that, from some cause or other, the health of Mrs. Anderton continued steadily to improve.

Matters had continued in this position for

some weeks, when objections were raised by
some of Mr. Anderton's relations to what
they not unnaturally considered the very
questionable propriety of the proceeding.
There seems to have been a good deal of
discussion on this point, in which, however,
Mr. Anderton's constitutional susceptibility
finally carried the day against his newly
conceived predilections with respect to a
practice so obviously calculated to expose
him to unpleasant comment. The Baron,
however, was not disposed so easily to relinquish a patient from whom he derived
such large and regular profits. On being
made acquainted with the decision respecting the cessation of his visits, he at once
declared that his own direct manipulations
were unnecessary, and that, if considered
improper for one of the opposite sex, they
could easily be made available at second-
hand.

Having once swallowed the original im-
position, any additional absurdity was of
course easily disposed of, and it was now
determined that, to avoid all occasion for

offence, Mrs. Anderton should henceforth be
operated upon through the medium of a certain Mademoiselle Rosalie, a 'clairvoyante'
in the employment of the Baron, who, after
being placed 'en rapport' with the patient,
was to convey to her the benefit of the manipulations to which she was herself subjected
by the operator.

Into the precise ' modus operandi ' I need
not now enter, but will only remark upon
the fresh instance of the extraordinary
powers of imagination displayed in the
still more rapid improvement of Mrs.
Anderton under this new form of treatment, and the marvellous 'sympathy' so
rapidly induced between her and the
Baron's 'medium.'

Mademoiselle Rosalie was a brunette,
rather below the medium height, with a
slight but beautifully proportioned and
active figure, sallow complexion, and dark
hair and eyes. The only fault a ' connois-
seur ' would probably find with her person
would be the extreme breadth of her feet,
though this might perhaps be accounted

for by her former occupation, to be noticed later on. It is necessary for our purpose that this peculiarity should be kept in mind. In appearance she was at that time about thirty years old, but might very possibly have been younger, as the nature of her profession would probably entail a premature appearance of age. Altogether she formed a remarkable contrast to Mrs. Anderton, who was slight but tall, and very fair, with remarkably small feet, and, notwithstanding her ill-health, still looking a year or two less than her age. Between these very different persons, however, if we are to credit the enclosed letters, such a 'sympathy' sprang up as would, on all ordinary hypotheses, be perfectly unaccountable. Mrs. Anderton could feel—or imagined that she felt—the approach of Mademoiselle Rosalie even before she entered the room; the mere touch of her hand seemed to afford immediate benefit, and within a very few weeks she became perfectly convalescent, and stronger than she had ever been before.

At this point I must again refer you to the depositions themselves; that of Mr. Morton, which here follows, being of too much importance to admit of condensation.

2. *Statement of Frederick Morton, Esq., late Lieutenant, R.A.*

My name is Frederick George Morton. In 1854 I was a lieutenant in the Royal Artillery, and was slightly wounded at the battle of Inkermann, on the 5th of November of that year, the day after my arrival in the Crimea. It was before joining the battery to which I was appointed. I have since quitted the service, on the death of my father, and am now residing with my mother at Leeds. I was an old school friend of the late Mr. William Anderton, and knew him intimately for nearly fifteen years. I was present at his marriage with Miss Boleton, in August 1851, and have since frequently visited at their house. During the time I was at Woolwich Academy, I spent every leave-out day with them, and frequently a good portion of the

vacation. My father encouraged the inti-
macy, and I was as much at home in their
house as in our own. My father was junior
partner of one of the large manufacturing
firms in Leeds. The Andertons generally
lived in London, when they were not
abroad; and on one occasion I went with
them to Wiesbaden. I saw very little of
them in 1854, as they were away the earlier
part of the year, first at Ilfracombe, and
then at Malvern, but I spent the 13th of
October with them. I particularly remember the date, as I was on my way to the
Crimea, where I was afterwards wounded,
and the order had come very suddenly.
When it came I had just gone to a friend's
house for some pheasant-shooting, and I
remember I was obliged to leave the second
morning, and I spent the night at Anderton's, and embarked the next morning. I
was to have gone for the first, but could
not get away, and I lost the shooting altogether. It was on a Saturday that I
embarked, because I remember we had
church parade next day. That was the

last time I saw Anderton. I was in Italy
all that winter with my wound and rheu-
matic fever; and in the summer of 1855 I
was sent to my father, who was ill for
several months before he died, and after
that I could not leave my mother. We
only took in a weekly paper, and I did not
hear of his having been taken up till three
or four days after. I started to see him
immediately, but was too late. It was not
on account of any quarrel that we had
not met. Quite the reverse. We were as
good friends as ever to the last, and I
would have given my life to serve him. I
was on the most friendly terms with Mrs.
Anderton. He was dotingly fond of her.
I used to laugh, and say I was jealous
of her, and they used to laugh too. I
never saw two people so fond of one
another. He was the best and kindest-
hearted fellow I ever knew, only awfully
nervous, and very sensitive about his
family and his name. The only time we
ever quarrelled was once at school, when
I tried to chaff him by pretending to

'Mrs Anderton lay on the sofa, and Rosalie sat on a chair by
her side, and held her hand while the Baron sent her to sleep.'

doubt something he had said: it made him quite ill. He often said he would rather die than have any stain upon his name, which he was very proud of. On the day I speak of—13th October, 1854 —I telegraphed to them at Notting Hill that I would dine and sleep there on my way out. I found Mrs. Anderton better than I had ever seen her before. She said it was all Baron R**'s doing, and that since Rosalie came she had got well faster than ever. She wanted to put off the Baron for that night, that we might have a quiet talk, but I would not let her; and, besides, I wanted to see him and Rosalie. They came at about nine o'clock, and Mrs. Anderton lay on the sofa, and Rosalie sat on a chair by her side, and held her hand while the Baron sent her to sleep. It was Rosalie he put to sleep, not Mrs. Anderton. The latter did not go to sleep, but lay quite still on the sofa, while Anderton and I sat together at the farther end of the room, because he said we might 'cross the mesmeric fluid.'

E

I don't know what he meant. Of course
I know that it was all nonsense; but I
don't think Rosalie was shamming. I
should go to sleep myself, if a man went
on that way. When it was over, Mrs.
Anderton said she felt much better, and I
couldn't help laughing; then Anderton
sent her up to bed, and he and I and the
Baron sat talking for an hour and more.
I never saw Mrs. Anderton again, for I
went away before she was up, but I used
to hear of her from Anderton. What we
talked of after she was gone was mesmerism. Of course I did not believe in
it, and I said so; and Anderton and
the Baron tried to persuade me it was
true. We were smoking, but Rosalie was
there, and said she did not mind it. She
always seemed to say whatever the Baron
wanted, but I don't think she liked him.
She did not join in the conversation. She
said—or at least the Baron said—she could
not speak English, but I am quite sure she
must have understood it, or at all events a
good deal. I have learned German, and

sometimes I said something to her, and she answered; and once I saw her look up so quickly when Anderton said something about ' Julie,' and the Baron said directly, in German, ' Not your Julie, child.' I asked her, as she was going away, who Julie was, and she had just told me that she was her great friend, and a dancing girl, when the Baron gave her a look, and she stopped. That was as they were leaving. Before that, Rosalie was doing crochet, and we three were talking about mesmerism. They tried to make me believe it, and the Baron was telling all sorts of stories about a wonderful ' clairvoyante.' That was his Julie, not Rosalie's. Of course I laughed at it all, and then they got talking about sympathies, and what a wonderful sympathy there was between twins, and the Baron told some more extraordinary stories. And when I wouldn't believe it, Anderton got quite vexed, and reminded me about the twin sister his wife had had, and who had been stolen by gipsies. And then the Baron asked him about it, and he told him

E 2

the whole story, only making him promise
not to tell it again, because they were
afraid of her being reminded of it, and
that was why it was never spoken of.
The Baron seemed quite interested, and
drew his chair close in between us. We
were speaking low, that Rosalie might not
hear. I remember the Baron said it was
so curious he must take a note of it, and
he wrote it all down in his pocket-book.
He took down the dates, and all about it.
He was very particular about the dates. I
am sure Rosalie could have heard nothing
of all this; not even if she had understood
English. We had gone to the window,
and were too far off. Besides, we spoke
low. Afterwards the Baron seemed thought-
ful, and did not speak for some time. Anderton and I got to mesmerism again, and
he got a number of some magazine—the
Zoïst, or something of that sort—to prove
to me something. He read me some wonderful story about eating by deputy, and
when I would not believe it, he called the
Baron and asked if it was not true, and he

said perfectly, he had known it himself.
He started when Anderton spoke to him, as
if he had been thinking of something else,
and he had to repeat it again.   I know
it was something about eating by deputy,
because afterwards, when I was wounded
and had the fever, I used to think of it,
and wish I could take physic that way.
You will find it in the *Zoïst* for that
month—October, 1854.*   I remember saying, at the time, that it was lucky for the
young woman that the fellow didn't eat
anything unwholesome, and Anderton
laughed at it.   The Baron did not laugh.
He stood for ever so long without saying
a word, and looking quite odd.   I thought
that I had offended him by laughing.   Anderton spoke to him, and he jumped again,
and I saw this time he had let his cigar
out.   I remember that, because he tried
to light it again by mine, and his hand
shook so he put mine out instead.   He
said he was cold, and shut the window.

* An extract from the magazine here quoted will
be given later on in the case.

He would not have another cigar, but said he must go away, for it was late. Anderton and I sat smoking for some time. I tried to persuade him to give up mesmerism, and he said Mrs. Anderton was so well now, he thought she could do without it, and that she would give it up in a few weeks. I heard from him afterwards, in November, that the Baron had left town for some weeks. When I was ill at Scutari, after my wound, I wrote to ask him to meet me at Naples, and he started with Mrs. Anderton in December, but was stopped at Dover by Mrs. Anderton's illness. I have had several letters from him since, and am quite ready to give copies of them; all but the bits that are private. I have read over this statement, and it is all quite true. I am quite ready to swear to it in a court of justice, if required. I wish to add that I am quite certain poor Anderton had nothing to do with his poor wife's death. I will swear to that.

3. *Statement of Julie.* *

'Manchester, Aug. 3, 1857.

' DEAR SIR,

'In compliance with your instructions
of the 11th ult., I forward deposition of
Julia Clark, *alias* Julie, *alias* Miss Montgomery, &c., at present of the Theatre
Royal, duly attested.

' Dear Sir,

' Yours faithfully,

'WILLIAM SMITH.'

'I am a dancer, and my name is Julia
Clark: I have performed under the name
of Julie, and other names. I am at present called Miss Montgomery. I knew the
girl called Rosalie. She was my particular
friend. We were for several years together
in Signor Leopoldo's company. I forget
how many. She did the tight-rope business,
and had two shillings a week and her keep.

* The difficulty of tracing this witness, from the
slight clue afforded by Mr. Morton's statement, occasioned considerable delay.

In our company she was called the 'Little Wonder.' Her real name was Charlotte Brown. She was about ten years old when I joined the company. I do not know her history. She did not know it herself. She often told me so. She would have told me if she did. She passed as the niece of old Mrs. Brown. Mrs. Brown was the money-taker. She took Lotty's money and found her in clothes. Lotty is Rosalie. Some of our ladies said she had been bought from a tramp. Of course I did not believe it. They said it out of spite. Lotty did the tight-rope business for about five years after I knew her. She was a beautiful figure, only her feet were very broad.* All tight-rope dancers' are. The rope spreads them. Otherwise her figure was perfect. She was nervous. Not very, but rather. She used to tremble before she went on. It was not from fear. She was ill some-times. Not often. Sometimes she caught cold from sitting on the damp ground to undress when she was hot with dancing.

* Section II., No. 1.

She got stronger as she grew up. Sometimes she felt ill, and did not know why.
She had bad headaches. When she was in
that way physic was no good, only brandy.
Brandy took away the headaches. She used
to drink brandy sometimes, but not like
some of our ladies. I never saw her the
worse for liquor. Her headaches were not
from drinking. Certainly not. They came
and went away again. Brandy took them
away. I only know of once that she has
been ill since she left the company. She
wrote and told me of it. I have the letter
still. It is not dated, but there was an
extract from a newspaper in it about her
which is dated some time in October,
1852.* The day of the month is cut off.
She gave up the tight-rope business because of a fall. That was from being
nervous. She was not drunk. She had
not been drinking. She was nervous. A
glass drop fell from the chandelier and
frightened her. That was all. She was
very much hurt. One foot was sprained,

* Section II., No. 1.

and the doctors at the hospital said she must never go on the wire again. She was two months there. When she came out the circus was shut up. The company was all dispersed except her and me and Mr. Rogers, and the gentleman who did the comic business. Mr. Rogers was Signor Leopoldo. He took a music-hall. I think it was in Liverpool. He got another singing lady and gentleman, and we gave entertainments. Every evening Mr. Rogers gave a short lecture on mesmerism, and Lotty was his subject. She was very clever at that. Of course she was not really asleep. One night she stopped in the middle. The manager was very angry. She tried to go on, but she fainted, and had to be carried off. She said some gentleman in the stalls had done it. Next morning the gentleman called and took her away. He gave the Signor 50*l*. He was the Baron R**. I knew it from Lotty. She has written to me several times. These are her letters. They are rubbed at the edges. It is from keeping them in my

pocket. I do not think she ever left the
Baron, but I do not know.   The last letter
I ever had from her was from his house.
It was in the first week of November,
1854. I got it in Plymouth. It was the
only week I was there before I went to
Dublin for the pantomime. She said she
was going to be married, but must not
tell me who to just yet. I never heard
from her since. I have written several
times, but my letters have been returned.
I have no idea who she married. It
could not have been the Baron. She disliked him too much. She stayed with him
because he paid her well. Partly that,
and partly because she said she couldn't
help doing what he told her. She said
he really did mesmerise her, and that
she could see in her sleep. She did not
live with the Baron as his wife. Only
as his medium. If she had she would
have told me. I am quite sure she would.
I am quite certain there was never any
connection between her and the Baron
except what I have said. Of course I

cannot swear she did not marry him, but I should think it very unlikely. Why should she when she disliked him so much? All this is true. I believe Signor Leopoldo is now somewhere abroad.

(Signed) ' JULIA CLARK, *alias* JULIE.'

Read over to the deponent, and signed by her in the presence of William Burton, J.P.

2nd August, 1857.

4. *Statement of Leopoldo.*

N.B.— This statement was obtained with some difficulty, and only on an express promise of immunity from any legal proceeding, in respect of the deponent's relations with the girl Rosalie, *alias* Angelina Fitz Eustace, *alias* the 'Little Wonder,' *alias* Charlotte Brown.   The statement was enclosed in the following note:—

'Signor Leopoldo, tragedian, &c. &c. &c., presents his compliments to R. Henderson, Esq., and in consideration of the assurance that " what is done cannot be now

amended," I have the honour to forward
the required information, in confidence that
you will not keep the word of promise to
the ear and break it to the hope, and thus
"my simple truth shall be abused."

 ' Sir, your most humble servant,
 (Signed)   ' THOMAS ROGERS.'

' Deposition of Signor Leopoldo, Tragedian;
 Professor of Fencing and Elocution;
 Equestrian, Gymnastic, and Funambulistic
 Artiste; Sole Proprietor and Manager of
 the Great Olympian Circus, &c. &c. &c.

 'I, Signor Leopoldo, tragedian, &c. &c.
&c., do hereby depose and declare that the
girl, Charlotte Brown, commonly known as
the celebrated ' Little Wonder,' was trans-
ferred by me to my celebrated Olympian
Company in the month of July, 1837, at
Lewes, in the county of Sussex, where the
celebrated Olympian Circus was at that
time performing with great success and
crowded houses. And this deponent further
maketh oath and saith that I, the said
Signor Leopoldo, tragedian, &c. &c. &c., did

in consideration of the services of the said
Charlotte Brown, commonly known as the
celebrated Little Wonder, pay to a certain
person or persons claiming to be the parent
or parents of the said Charlotte Brown,
commonly known as the celebrated Little
Wonder, the sum of five pounds (5*l.*), which
person or persons were of the tribe or tribes
commonly known as gipsies or Egyptians.
And this deponent furthermore maketh oath
and saith that I, Signor Leopoldo, tragedian, &c. &c. &c., cannot tell whether the
said Charlotte Brown, commonly known as
the Little Wonder, was really the child of
the person or persons, gipsy or gipsies
aforesaid, or that her name was Charlotte
Brown, or any other of the particulars
hereinbefore stated and deposed, but only
that her linen was marked C. B., which
initials do set forth and represent the name
of Charlotte Brown.

'Witness our hand and seal this fourth
day of January, in the year of grace, one
thousand eight hundred and fifty-eight.

  (Signed) 'THOMAS ROGERS.'

5. *Statement of Edward Morris, Clerk in
    the Will Office, Doctors' Commons.*

'My name is Edward Morris. I am a
clerk in the Will Office at Doctors' Commons, and my duty is to assist those who
wish to search wills deposited in our office.
On the 14th October, 1854, Baron R**
came to the office and searched in several
wills. One was the will of a Mr. Wilson,
copy of which is herewith enclosed. I remember this will particularly, because I
had an altercation with the Baron respecting his wish to copy parts of it. He
wished to make extracts, and I told him it
was not allowed; only the date and names
of the executors. He persisted, and I said
I must report it. He then laughed, and
said it did not matter, and he tapped his
forehead and said he could make a note of
it there. He read parts of the will over
two or three times, and gave it back to me.
He then said, "You shall see, my friend,"
and laughed again, and he made me follow
him while he repeated several pages of the
will by rote. He laughed again when he

had done, and asked if he might copy it now. I said no: and he laughed again, and wrote for some time in his note-book, looking up at me every now and then and laughing. I was angry, partly because he laughed, and partly because he kept me there when I wanted to get away. I had leave for a week to go to the Isle of Wight and see my aunt. I wanted to get there that night, because the next day was my birthday. He made me miss the train, and as the next day was Sunday, I did not get there till late. That is how I remember the date. I am sure of the year, because my aunt only went to the Isle of Wight the November previously, and died in the spring of 1855. I am quite sure it was the Baron. I should recognise him anywhere. He is a short, stout man, with a rather florid complexion and reddish hair, rather light. He has large fat hands, white and well kept, and an immense head. He dresses all in black, and wears large spectacles of light blue. I don't think it is because his eyes are weak. I am sure it is not; for

when he takes off his spectacles I never
saw such extraordinary eyes. I can't describe them, only that they are very large
and bright. I never could look at them
long enough to make out the colour, but
they are very dark, I think black, and they
put one out to look at them, otherwise
there is nothing very remarkable about him.
I recognised him that day from having
seen him before at a mesmeric lecture,
when I asked his name.'

6. *Memorandum by Mr. Henderson.*

I enclose the will of which the following
is an abstract:—

'Mr. Wilson, of the firm of Price &
Wilson, Calcutta, who died in 1825, leaves
the sum of 25,375*l.* three per cent. consols,
to his niece Gertrude Wilson (afterwards
Lady Boleton), and to her children, if any,
or their heirs in regular succession, whether
male or female. In default of any such
heirs, the money to be made over to trus-
tees selected by the Governor General of
India for the time being, from among the

leading merchants of Calcutta, for the purpose of founding, under certain restrictions,
an institution among the hills for the children of those who could not afford to send
them home to England.'

The will also provides that should any
female taking under it die during her cover-
ture, the husband shall retain a life interest
in the property.

SECTION III.

1. *Extracts from Mrs. Anderton's Journal.*

Aug. 13, 1854.—Here we are, then, finally established at Notting Hill. Jane laughs at us for coming to town just as every one else is leaving it; but in my eyes, and I am sure in dear William's too, that is the pleasantest time for us. Poor Willie, he grows more and more sensitive to blame from any one, and has been sadly worried by this discussion about our Dresden trip. The new professor to-morrow. I wonder what he will be like.

Aug. 14.—And so *that* is the new professor! I do not think I was ever so astonished in my life. That little stout squab man, the most powerful mesmerist in Europe! And yet he certainly is powerful, for he had scarcely made a pass over me before I felt a glow through my whole frame. There is something about him, too, when one comes to look at him more closely, which puzzles me very much. He certainly is not the common-place man he appears, though it would be difficult just now to say what makes me so sure of it.

Aug. 25.—Quite satisfied now. How could I have ever thought the Baron common-place! And yet, at first sight, his appearance is certainly against him. He is not a man with whom I should like to quarrel. I don't think he would have much compunction in killing any one who offended him, or who stood in his way. How quietly he talks of those horrid experiments in the medical schools, and the tortures they inflict on the poor hospital patients. Willie says it is all nonsense, and says all doctors talk so; but I can't help feeling that there is something different about him. And yet he is certainly doing me good.

Sept. 1.—Better and better, and yet I cannot conquer the strange feeling which is growing upon me about the Baron. He is certainly an extraordinary man. What a grasp he takes of anything on which he rests his hand even for a moment; and how perfectly he seems to disregard anything that stands in his way. This morning I was at the window when he came, and I was quite frightened when I saw him, as I thought, so nearly run over. But I might have spared my anxiety, for my gentleman just walked quietly on, while the poor horse started almost across the road. Had it caught sight of those wonderful green eyes of his, that it seemed so frightened? What eyes they are! You can hardly ever see them; but when you do!—And yet the man is certainly doing me good.

Sept. 11.—So it is settled that the Baron is not to mesmerise me himself any more. Am I sorry or glad? At all events, I hope they will not now worry poor William. . .

Sept. 13.—First day of Mademoiselle Rosalie. Seems a nice person enough; but it feels very odd to lie there on the sofa while some one else is being mesmerised for one.

Sept. 15.—This new plan is beginning

to answer. I think I feel the mesmerism even more than when I was mesmerised myself, and this way one gets all the pleasures and none of the disagreeables. It *is* so delicious. Looked back to-day at my Malvern journals. So odd to see how I disliked the idea at first, and now I could hardly live without it.

Sept. 29.—I think we shall soon be able to do .without the Baron altogether. I am sure Rosalie and I could manage very well by ourselves. What a wonderful thing this mesmerism is! To think that the mere touch of another person's hand should soothe away pain, and fill one with health and strength. Really, if I had not always kept a journal, I should feel bound to keep one now, as a record of the wonderful effects of this extraordinary cure. Got up this morning with a nasty headache. No appetite for breakfast. Eyes heavy, and pulse low. Poor William in terrible tribulation, when lo! in comes little Mademoiselle Rosalie and the Baron. The gentleman makes a pass or two—the lady pops her little, dry, monkey-looking paw upon my forehead, and, *presto*! the headache has vanished, and I'm calling for chocolate and toast.

Sept. 30.—A blank day. Headache again this morning, and looking out anxiously for my little brown ' good angel,' when in comes the Baron, with the news that she cannot come. Up all night with a dying lady, and so fagged this morning that he is afraid she would do me more harm than good. I am sure she cannot feel more fagged than I do, poor girl. But, after all, in spite of the delight of doing so much good, what a life it must be!

Oct. 1.—Rosalie here again. Headache vanished. Everything bright as the October sun outside. I am getting quite fond of that girl. How I wish she could speak something besides German.   .   .   .

Oct. 4.—It is quite extraordinary what a hold that poor girl, Rosalie, is taking upon me. I am even beginning to dream of her at night.   .   .   .

Oct. 6.—Headache again this morning, and a message that Rosalie cannot come.

How provoking that it is on the same
day.   .   .   .

Oct. 12.—I think I shall really soon begin
to know when poor Rosalie has been over-
worked.   Headache again to day, and I had
a presentiment that she would not be able
to come.   .   .   .

Oct. 20.*—So now the Baron is going to
leave us.   Well, I am indeed thankful that
he can now so well be spared.   Jane Morgan here to-day, and of course laughing at
the idea of mesmerism doing any good.
She could not deny, though, how wonderfully better I am; and, indeed, but for those
tiresome headaches, which always seem to
come just when poor Rosalie is too tired
to take them away, I am really quite well
and strong.

Oct. 31.—Something evidently wrong
between poor Rosalie and the Baron.   She
has evidently been crying, and I suppose it
must be from sympathy, but I feel exactly
as if I had been crying too.   Very little
satisfaction from the mesmerism to-day.

* Compare Section II., 2 and 5.

It seems rather as if it had given me some of poor Rosalie's depression. How I wish she could speak English, or that I could speak German, and then I would find out what is the matter. Perhaps she is to lose her work when the Baron goes. Mem.: To ask him to-morrow.

Nov. 1.—No. He says he shall certainly take her with him to Germany, and 'he hopes that may have a beneficial effect.' What can he mean? He says she is quite well, but throws out mysterious insinuations as to something being wrong with her. How I do wish I could speak German.

Nov. 3.—Still that uncomfortableness between the Baron and Rosalie. I am sure there is something wrong, and that she wants to speak to me about it, but is afraid of him. It certainly is strange that he should never leave us alone. Mem.: To ask William to get him out of the way for a little while to-morrow, though what good that will be when she and I cannot understand each other, I hardly know after all. . . .

Nov. 4.—What a day this has been! I feel quite tired out with the excitement, and yet I cannot make up my mind to go to bed until I have written it all down. In the first place, this is to be my last visit from Rosalie; at all events till they come back from the continent. I cannot help perceiving that William is not altogether sorry that she is going. Dear fellow! I do really believe that he is more than half jealous of my extraordinary feeling for her. And certainly it is extraordinary that a woman quite in another class of life, of whom one knows nothing, should have taken such a hold upon one. I suppose it must be the mesmerism, which certainly is a very mysterious thing. If it is so, it is at all events very fortunate it did not take that turn with the Baron himself. Ugh! I can really begin to understand now all the objections I thought so foolish and so tiresome three or four months ago, before Rosalie first came. And yet, after all, I don't think—in spite of mesmerism or anything else—one need ever have been afraid of

liking the Baron too much.   I could quite
understand being afraid of him.   Rosalie
evidently is, and to own the truth so am I
a little, or I should not have been beaten
in that way to-day.   To-day was my last
'séance' with Rosalie, and I had made up
my mind to get the Baron out of the way,
and try and get something out of Rosalie.
They came at two o'clock as usual, and as
I thought I would not lose a chance, I had
got dear William to lie in wait in his study,
and call to the Baron as he passed, in hopes
that Rosalie would come up alone.   That
was no use, however, for the Baron kept
his stout little self perseveringly between
her and the staircase, and when I went—
thinking to be very clever—to the top of
the staircase and called to her to come up,
it only gave him an excuse for breaking
away from poor William altogether, and
coming straight up to me before her.   I
was so provoked I could hardly be civil.
Well, of course the Baron was in a great
hurry, and we went to work at once with
the mesmerising.   When that was done,

we both tried to keep them talking, and I
made signs to William to get the Baron out
of the way. I was really beginning to get
quite anxious about it, and kept on repeat-
ing over and over to myself the two German words I had learned on purpose from
Jane Morgan this morning. It was no
use, however, and I began to grow quite
nervous; and I am quite sure Rosalie saw
what I was wanting, for she seemed to get
fidgety too, and then that made me more
nervous still. At last the Baron declared
he must go, and they both got up to leave.
William would have given it up, but he
says I looked so imploringly at him he could
not resist, so made one more effort by asking the Baron to come into his study for a
short private consultation. This he refused,
saying he had not time, but could say anything needful were they were. Then William told me to take Rosalie into the next
room, but the Baron would not have that
either, though he laughed when he said he
could not trust to a lady's punctuality in
this case, but if I would leave Rosalie she

would not understand anything that was said. Of course this would not do, and at last William, with more presence of mind and determination than I should have thought him capable of, took him by the button-hole and fairly drew him away into the further window, where he began whispering eagerly to him to draw off his attention. I suppose it was the consciousness of a sort of stratagem, but my heart beat quite fast as I brought out my two words, ' Gibst' was?' and I could see that hers was so too. She seemed surprised at my speaking to her in German, and certainly I was no less so to hear her answer in English, with a slight accent certainly, but still in quite plain English—' Don't seem to listen. I am . . .' and then she stopped suddenly and turned quite pale, and I could feel all my own blood rush back to my heart with such a throb! I looked up, and there were the Baron's eyes fixed upon us. Poor Rosalie seemed quite frightened, and I declare I felt so too. At all events, we neither of us ventured on another word, and the next minute the Baron succeeded in fairly shaking off poor William and taking his leave. So there is an end of my little romance about Rosalie. I am *sure* there was something in it. Why, if she had nothing particular to say, should she have taken the trouble of learning that little bit of English? and why—but I must not sit here all night speculating about this, which after all is, I dare say, nothing at all. It is positively just twelve o'clock.

Nov. 6.—How strange! There is certainly some mystery about Rosalie and the Baron. I am quite certain I saw them in a cab together this morning, and yet they were to cross on Saturday night and be in Paris yesterday. I wonder whether they were late after all, and yet an hour and a-half is surely time enough to London Bridge, and if he had missed the train I should think he would have come to us yesterday. At all events he might have gone early this morning. It is very odd. . . .

Nov. 7.—I wonder whether any one ever

had such a husband as I have got.   Yesterday he must needs worry himself with the
idea that I am fretting about the loss of my
mesmerism,—as if I could possibly think a
moment about the loss of anything when
I had got him with me.   So nothing would
satisfy him but that we must go to the Hay-
market to see 'Paul Pry' and the Spanish
Dancers.   I have not laughed so much for
many a long day.   I don't like all that
violent dancing, so we came away directly
after the absurd little farce—'How to Pay
the Rent.'   How we did laugh at it to be
sure, and the absurdities of that little
monkey, Clark.   Wright, too, in 'Paul
Pry,' is quite inimitable.   Dear William,
how good it was of him! . . . .

Dec. 5.—Just going to the theatre again
when news came of poor Harry Morton's
illness.   My own dear William, how good
he is to every one.   And so prompt, too.
Touch his heart or his honour, and the
Duke himself could not be more quick and
decided.   The news only came as we were
dressing, and to-morrow we are off to

Naples to meet poor Mr. Morton, and nurse him.

Dec. 6.—There is no one like Willie. After all the scramble we have had to get ready, he would not take me across when it was so rough. So we have taken two dear little rooms, from day to day, because Willie cannot bear the publicity of an hotel, and I am sure I hate it too, and we are to wait till it is fine enough to cross.

Dec. 9.—Still here; but the wind has gone down almost suddenly within the last three hours, and to-morrow morning I hope we really shall cross. Dear William getting quite worried; I persuaded him to take me to a lecture that was going on, and while we were there the wind went down, and we have been packing up ever since. Twelve o'clock! and William calling to me. I *must* just put down about Mr. . . . Good Heaven! What is the matter? I feel so ill—quite—

2.—*Statement of Dr. Watson.*

'My name is James Watson, and I am a

physician of about thirty years' standing. In 1854, I was practising at Dover. On the night of the 9th of December in that year, I was sent for hurriedly to see a lady, of the name of Anderton, who had been taken suddenly ill immediately after her return from a lecture at the Town-hall, which she had attended with her husband. The message was brought by the servant from the lodgings where they were living. On our way to the house she told me that "the lady was dying, and the poor gentleman quite distracted." On arriving at the house I found Mr. Anderton supporting his wife in his arms. He seemed greatly agitated and cried, "For God's sake be quick— I think she has got the cholera!"

[N.B.—The following portion of Dr. Watson's statement, relating entirely to the symptoms of Mrs. Anderton's case, though some details are excluded, and others described as far as possible in non-medical terms, necessarily contains much that must be interesting only to the medical profession, and disagreeable to the general reader. The following paragraph may therefore be passed over, merely noting that the symptoms were such as would be developed in a case of antimonial poisoning.]

' Mrs. Anderton was on the couch in her dressing-room, partially undressed, but with two or three blankets thrown over her, as she seemed shivering with the cold. There was a good fire in the room, but notwithstanding this and the blankets, her hands and feet were both quite chilly. I asked Mr. Anderton why she had not been got to bed, to which he replied, that she had been, until within a very few moments, so violently sick, that they had been unable to move her. Almost immediately on my arrival this disturbance re-commenced, though there appeared to be now hardly anything left in the stomach. The sickness continued with unabated violence for more than an hour after the stomach had been evidently completely emptied, and was accompanied with other internal derangement and severe cramps both in the stomach and the extremities. I at once sent to my house for a portable bath I happened to have hired for my own wife's use, and on its arrival, placed Mrs. Anderton in it at a temperature of 98°, having previously

'On arriving at the house I found Mr Anderton supporting his wife in his arms... Mrs Anderton was on the couch in her dressing-room, partially undressed, but with two or three blankets thrown over her, as she seemed shivering with the cold.'

added three quarters of a pound of mustard. While waiting for the bath, I administered thirty drops of laudanum in a wine-glassful of hot brandy-and-water, but without, in any degree, checking the symptoms before mentioned, which continued almost incessantly. They were accompanied also by violent pains and great swelling of the 'epigastrium.' A fresh dose of opium was equally unsuccessful, nor was any amelioration of symptoms produced by the exhibition of prussic acid and creosote. On removing the patient from the warm bath, I had her carefully placed in bed, shortly after which she began to perspire profusely, but without any relief to the other symptoms.

[The narrative here recommences.]

'I now began to fear that some deleterious substance had been swallowed, more especially as the patient had, up to the very moment of her seizure, been in unusually good health. I therefore made careful examinations with the view to detecting the presence of arsenic; and instituted, by the

aid of Mr. Anderton, the strictest enquiries
as to whether there was in the house any
preparation containing this or any other
irritant poison. Nothing of the kind could,
however, be found, nor were such tests, as I
was at the time in a position to apply, able
to detect anything of the kind to which
my suspicions were directed. Deliberate
poisoning proved, moreover, on consideration, entirely out of the question, as there
could be no doubt of Mr. Anderton's devoted attachment to his wife, and the people of the house were entire strangers to
her. Moreover, the length of time since
any food had been taken was almost conclusive against such a supposition. Mrs.
Anderton had dined at six o'clock, and between that hour and midnight, when the
attack came on, had eaten nothing but a
biscuit and part of a glass of sherry-and-
water, the remainder of which was in the
glass upon the dressing-room table when I
arrived. Since then I have removed portions of all the matters tested, as well as the
remaining wine-and-water, and have had

them thoroughly examined by a scientific
chemist, but equally without result. I am
compelled, therefore, to believe that the
symptoms arose from some natural, though
undiscovered cause. Possibly from a sudden chill in coming from the heated rooms
into the night air, though this seems hardly
compatible with the fact that she never
complained of cold during the long drive
home, and that she was seated comfortably
in her dressing-room, making her customary
entries in her journal, when the attack
came on. Another very suspicious circumstance was that, afterwards mentioned by
her, of a strong metallic taste in the mouth,
a symptom sometimes occasioned, and in
conjunction likewise with the others noticed
in her case, by the exhibition of excessive
doses of antimony in the form of emetic
tartar. This medicine, however, had never
been prescribed for her, nor was there any
possibility of her having had access to any
in mistake. At Mr. Anderton's request,
however, I exhibited the remedies used in
such a case, as port wine, infusion of oak-

bark, &c., but with as little effect as the other medicines. Indeed, the remedies of whatever kind were precluded from exercising their full action by the extreme irritability of the stomach, by which they were rejected almost as soon as swallowed. This being the case, I abandoned any further attempt at the exhibition of the heavy doses I had hitherto employed, or indeed of drugs of any kind, and confined myself, until the irritation of the 'epigastrium' should have been in some measure allayed, to a treatment I have occasionally found successful in somewhat similar cases; the administration, that is to say, of simple soda-water in repeated doses of a teaspoonful at a time. I have often found this to remain with good effect upon the stomach when everything else was at once rejected, nor was I disappointed in the present case. About an hour after commencing this treatment, the first violence of the symptoms began to subside, and by the next afternoon the case had resolved itself into an ordinary one of severe 'gastro-enteritis,' which I then proceeded to treat in the regular manner. After quite as short a period as I could possibly have expected, this also was subdued, leaving the patient, however, in a state of great prostration, and subject to night-perspirations of the most lowering character. I now began to throw in tonics, and to resort, though very cautiously, to more invigorating diet. Under this treatment she continued steadily to improve, though the perspirations still continued, and her constitution cannot be said to have at all recovered the severe shock it had sustained by the month of April 1855, when they left Dover, by my recommendation, for change of air. Since that time I have not seen her. I am quite unable to account for the seizure from any cause but that of a chill; an hypothesis which, I must admit, rests its authority almost solely on the fact that no other can be found.'

*3. Extracts from Mrs. Anderton's Journal
—continued.*

Jan. 20, 1855.—At last I get back once
more to my old brown friend.* Dear old
thing, how pleasant its old face seems!
Very little to-day, though; only a word or
two, just to say it is done. Oh, how it
tries one.

Jan. 25.—My own dear husband's birthday; and, thank Heaven! I am once more
able to sit with him. Oh! how kind he
has been through all these weary weeks,
when I have been so fretful and impatient.
Why should suffering make one cross?
God knows, I *have* suffered. I never
thought to live through that terrible night.
It makes me shudder to think of it. And,
then, that horrid, deathlike, leaden taste—
that was worst of all. Well, thank God!
I am better now, but *so* weak. I am quite
tired with writing even these few lines. . .

Feb. 12.—How weak I still am! Walked
out to-day with dear William, for the first

* Apparently the journal, which is bound in brown
Russian leather.

time, upon the pier; but had scarcely got to
the end of it, when I felt so tired I was
obliged to sit down, while poor William
went to fetch a chair to take me home.

Feb. 13.—I have been quite startled to-
day. I was talking to Dr. Watson about
my being so tired yesterday, and about
how very weak I still was, and how ill I
had been—and, at last, he let slip that, at
the time, he thought I had been poisoned.
It gave me quite a turn, and then he tried
to make us talk of something else; but I
could not get it out of my head, and kept
coming back and back to it, and wondering
who could have had any possible interest in
poisoning poor me. And so we went on
talking; and, at last Dr. Watson said something which let out that at first he had
suspected—William! my own William! my
precious, precious husband! Oh! I thought
I should have choked on the spot. I don't
know what I said, but I do know I could
not have said too much, and poor William
tried to laugh it off, and said: ' Who else
would have gained anything by it? Would

he not have had that miserable 25,000*l.*?
and besides him, there was no one but the
Charities in India, and they could not have
done it, because they would not exist till
we were gone;' but I could see how he
winced at the idea, and I felt as though my
blood were really boiling in my veins.   And
then that man—oh! how thankful I shall
be when we can get away from him—tried to
persuade me that he had not really thought
it.   I should think not, indeed! and that
he soon saw it was impossible, and all that;
and at last, I fairly burst out crying with
passion, and ran out of the room.   And—
and—I could cry now to think of my poor
dear Willie being—and I shall, too, if I go
on thinking about it any longer, so I will
write no more to-night.

Feb. 15.—No journal yesterday : I really
could not trust myself to write.   And poor
Willie, though he tried to laugh at it, I
could see how bitterly he felt the imputation.   Good Heaven! think if that wretched
man had really charged him with it.   It
would have killed him.   I know it would,

and he would rather have died a thousand times. Well, I must not think of it any more. Only, once more, thank Heaven! we shall soon be going away.

April 7.—Back once more at home, thank Heaven! But how slow, how very slow this convalescence, as they call it, is. Oh! shall I ever be well again, as I was last year before that horrid day at Dover?

May 3.—So we are to leave England for a time, and try the German baths. I am almost thankful for it. I have grown very fond, too, of this dear little luxurious house, though I could hardly say why. It is like my wonderful fancy for Rosalie. Ah, poor Rosalie! I wonder where she is now, and when they will return. I cannot help thinking she might do me some good. But, as I was saying, fond as I am of this dear little house, I shall be really glad to leave it for a time, and see what change of air will do for me. If I could only get rid of those terrible night perspirations. It is they that pull me down so, and make me so weak and miserable. Oh! what would

I not give to be well once more, if it were only to get rid of the memory of that time.

July 7.—Safe at Baden Baden; and too early as yet for the majority of the English pleasure-seekers. What a delicious place it is; I declare I quite feel myself better already. . . .

Sept. 11.—Really almost well again. Quite a comfortable talk to-day with dear Willie about that foolish Dr. Watson; the first time the subject has been mentioned between us, since that day when I got into such a passion about it. Poor man, he was hardly worth going into a rage about. We heard to-day of his having made some terrible blunder in the new place he has gone to, and lost all his practice by killing some poor old woman through it. It was this made us talk of his poisoning notion, and oh! how glad I was to see that dear Willie had quite got over his nervousness about it. We had quite a long talk; and, at last, he promised me faithfully never to say a word more about it to any one.

Oct. 10.—Home again at last, and in

our own dear little house. And really I
feel once more as well and strong as this
time last year. Dear William, too, how
happy he is; the shadow seems quite to have
passed away. God grant it may not return.

Oct. 30.—An eventful day. All the
morning at the Crystal Palace, and just as
we returned who should walk in but the
Baron R**! It was just a year since he
left us, but he had not altered in the very
least. I do not think that short, square
figure, with the impenetrable rosy face,
and the large white hands, and those wonderful great green eyes that you can so
rarely catch, and when you have caught,
so invariably wish you had let alone, can
ever change. I am afraid I was not very
cordial to him. I ought to be, for he has
done great things for me; and yet somehow
when I saw him, I felt quite a cold shudder
run all through me. Dear William saw it,
and asked if I was ill, and when I laughed
and said, ' No, it was only some one walking over my grave,' I could not help
fancying that for a moment the Baron's

lips seemed to turn quite white, and I just
caught one glance from those awful eyes
that seemed as if it would read me through
and through. And yet after all it may
have been only fancy, for the next moment
he was talking in his rich, quiet voice as
though nothing could ever disturb him.
So Rosalie is gone. That is clear at all
events, though what has exactly become of
her I cannot quite so well understand.
From all I can make out, she seems, poor
girl to have married very foolishly, and it
was that that was the matter between them
when they went away last year. The
Baron seemed indeed to hint at something
even worse, but he would not speak out
plainly, and I would defy any one to make
that man say one word more than he may
choose. Poor Rosalie, I hope she has not
come to any harm.

Nov. 1.—Another visit from the Baron,
to say good-bye before his return to—his
wife! How strange that we should never
have heard of her before, and even now I
cannot make out whether he has married

since he left us or whether he was always so. Certainly that man is a mystery, and just now it pleases him to talk especially in enigmas. He does not seem disposed, however, to put up with vague information on our part. I thought he would never have done questioning poor William and me about my illness, and at last he drew it out of me—not out of William, dear fellow—what that foolish Dr. Watson had said. After all I am not sorry I told him, for it was quite a relief to hear him speak so strongly of the absurdity of such an idea, and I am sure it was a comfort to poor William. He—the Baron—spoke very strongly too about the danger of setting such ideas about, and particularly cautioned dear Willie not to mention it to any one. I knew he would not have done so any way, but this will make him more comfortable.

April 3.—Such a delightful day, and so tired. I never saw Richmond look so lovely, and how dear Willie and I did enjoy ourselves in that lovely park. But, oh! I am so sleepy. Not a word more.

April 5.—Another lovely day—strolling about Lord Holland's Park all the morning, and this evening some music in our own dear little drawing-room. How happy—how very happy—good Heaven, what is this? That old horrible leaden taste; and oh, so deadly sick. . . .

April 6.—Thank heaven, the attack seems to have passed away. Oh, how it frightened me. Thank heaven, too, I was able to keep the worst from dear William, and he did not know how like it was to that other dreadful time.

April 20.—Again that horrible sickness, and worse—oh, far worse—still, that awful deadly leaden taste. Worse this time, too, than the last. In bed all day yesterday. Poor Willie terribly anxious. Pray Heaven it may not come again.

May 6.—Another attack. God help me! if this should go on, I do not know what will become of me. Already I am beginning to feel weaker and weaker. Poor Willie!—these last three days have been terrible ones for him. However, the doctor says it will all pass off. Pray Heaven it may!

May 25.—More sickness, more derangement, more of that horrible leaden taste. The doctor himself is beginning to look uncomfortable, and I can see that poor Willie's mind is reverting to that terrible suggestion a year ago. Thank Heaven, I have as yet managed to conceal from him and from Dr. Dodsworth that horrid deadly taste which made such an impression on Dr. Watson. Oh! when will this end?

June 10.—A horrible suspicion is taking possession of me. What can this mean? I look back through my journal, and it is every fortnight that this fearful attack returns. The 5th and 18th of April—3rd and 21st of May—and now again the 7th of this month. And that terrible leaden taste which is now almost constantly in my mouth; and with every attack my strength failing—failing—O God, what can it be?

June 26.—Another fortnight—another attack. There *must* be foul play somewhere. And yet who could—who would do such a thing? Thank Heaven, I have still concealed from my poor William that worst symptom of all, the horrible leaden taste which is now never out of my mouth. My precious Willie, how kind, how good he is to me.   .   .   .   .

July 12.—I cannot hold out much longer now. Each time the attack returns I lose something of the little, the very little strength that is left. God help me, I feel now that I must go. . . . The Baron came to-day, and for a moment my poor boy's face lighted up with hope again. They had a long discussion before the doctor would consent to consult with him, but after that, they seemed to change the medicines. But something must have gone wrong, for I have never seen Dr. Dodsworth look so grave.

Aug. 1.—I think the end is drawing very near now. This last attack has weakened me more than ever, and I write this in my bed. I shall never rise from it again. My poor, poor Willie . . Three days I have been in bed now, but I have taken nothing from any hand but his.

Aug. 17.—This is, I think, almost the the last entry I shall make. Another fortnight and I shall be too weak to hold the pen—if, indeed, I am still here.

Sept. 5.—Another attack. Strange how this weary body bears up against all this pain. Would that it were over; and yet my poor, poor boy. . . He too, is almost worn out: night and day he never leaves me. . . . I take the things from his hand, but I cannot taste them now—nothing but lead. . . .

Sept. 27.*—Farewell, my husband—my darling—my own precious Willie. Think of me—come soon to me. God bless you —God comfort you—my darling—my own.

In the hand of Mr. Anderton.

This day my darling died.
Oct. 12th, 1856.   W. A.

* Written in pencil, the characters barely legible from weakness.

SECTION IV.

1. *Memorandum by Mr. Henderson.*

In the following certificate * you will see
that the lady therein mentioned is described as of ' Acacia Cottage, Kensington.'
The identity of the name with that given by
Julie and Leopoldo, as the proper designation
of the Baron's ' medium,' confirmed my suspicion that it was in fact to the girl Rosalie
that the Baron was married under that
name, notwithstanding the strong opinion
of Julie as to the impossibility of such being
the case. Still, however, it was possible
that this might, after all, be a mere coincidence; and I therefore proceeded to make
such enquiries as seemed most likely to
elucidate the point. I had considerable
difficulty in finding the house, which two

* See next page.

CERTIFICATE.

1854. *Marriage solemnised at the Parish Church in the Parish of Kensington, in the County of Middlesex.*

No.	Date.	Name and Surname.	Age.	Condition.	Rank or Profession.	Residence.	Father's Name.	Rank or Profession of Father.
61	6 Nov. 1854.	Carl Schwartz.	Full age.	Bachelor.	Gentleman.	Windermere Villas, Notting Hill.	Carl Schwartz.	Gentleman.
		Charlotte Brown.	Full age.	Spinster.		Acacia Cottage.	Not known.	Not known.

Married in the Parish Church according to the rites and ceremonies of the Established Church, *after banns*, by me

J. W. EDWARDS, B.A.

This marriage was solemnised } CARL SCHWARTZ,   In the presence of us, } THOMAS JONES,
between us,   } CHARLOTTE BROWN,   } FREDERICK COLEMAN.

The above is a copy from the Register of Marriages belonging to this Church. Witness my hand, 7th day of November, 1854.

R. JOHNSON.

or three years back was included in the
regular numbering of the row of similar
tenements in which it stands; but I at last
succeeded in identifying it. I found the
landlady a very deaf old person, whose
memory was evidently failing, and was at
first unable to extract from her any kind
of information on the subject, except that
'she had had a great many lodgers, and
couldn't be expected to know all about all
of them.' In the course of a second visit,
however, I succeeded in persuading her to
favour me with a sight of her books, and
looking back to October and November
1854, I found the sum of 2*l.* 5*s.*, entered
as payment from Miss C. Brown of three
weeks' rent, from the 18th of October to
the 8th of November.* On further examining the books, I found that at this time,
while the other lodger was charged sundry
sums for fire, Miss Brown, though occupying the principal sitting-room, had no fire
at all during the whole time of her tenancy,
though the commencement of November

* Compare Sections II., 2 and 5, and III., 1.

in that year was unusually cold.   There
were also sundry other little charges in-
variable in the other cases, but omitted in
the case of Miss Brown; and at length, on
these things being pointed out to her, the
old lady managed to remember that the
rooms had been taken by a gentleman for
a lady who was to give lessons in drawing.   The gentleman had paid the three
weeks' rent in advance, and had specially
requested that they might be kept vacant
for her, as the time of her arrival was
uncertain.   He had also begged that any
letters or messages received for her should
be sent to a certain address immediately.
After a great deal of searching, this address was at length found, and proved to
be the square glazed card which I enclose.

2. *'Letters or messages for Miss Brown
to be forwarded immediately to care of*

'𝕭𝖆𝖗𝖔𝖓 ℝ**,

'*Post Office, Notting Hill.*'

The old lady further stated that she
never saw the gentleman again and that

she had never seen the lady at all. In fact,
after payment of the money, nothing
further had been heard of either of the
parties concerned; and as no enquiries
had been made for Miss Brown, the subject had altogether passed from her mind.

Being thus pretty well satisfied of the
identity of Madame R**, my next care
was to trace the proceedings of the Baron
between the time of his marriage and the
death of his wife, which took place, as
you are aware, in London, about two
years and a half subsequently; the insurances having, as you well know, been
effected at about the middle of this period.
The information afforded me by Dr. Jones,
the medical man who signed the certificate
to your office in connection with the policy
on the life of Madame R**, first gave me
the required clue, and you will, I think,
find in the depositions immediately following, sufficient, at all events, to justify
if not entirely to corroborate, the suspicions which first gave rise to my enquiries.   It is certainly unfortunate that

here, too—as in the case of Mr. Aldridge,
whose letter first aroused these suspicions
— the witness on whose evidence the
principal stress must be laid, is not one
whose testimony would probably carry
much weight with a jury.   Such, however,
as it is, I have felt it my duty to lay it
before you; and I will now leave it, with
such other as I have been able to collect,
to tell its own tale.

3.—*Statement of Mrs. Whitworth.*

'My name is Jane Whitworth.   I am a
widow, and gain my living by letting
furnished apartments at Bognor, Sussex.
The principal season at Bognor is during
the Goodwood races, and there are very
few visitors there in the autumn and winter.   On the 6th November, 1854, I let the
whole upper part of my house to a lady
and gentleman, who arrived there late that
evening.   They gave some foreign name;
I forget what.   It was some queer German
name.   They did not give the name at
first.   Not till I asked for it.   I don't

know that the gentleman was particularly
unwilling. I said I wanted it for my
bill; and he laughed, and said it did not
matter,—anything would do. Then I said,
if letters came, and he said:—' Oh! there
won't be any letters,' and went on reading
the paper. I went down stairs, and as I
was going down he rang, and I went back,
and he told me of his own accord. That
was at the end of the first week when I
was making out my bill. They said they
intended remaining for some weeks. It
was the gentleman who said this. The
lady took no part in the business, and
seemed out of spirits, and very much afraid
of her husband. He settled with me to
take the apartments at thirty shillings
a week. He was to remain as long as
he liked. Not beyond the next race week,
of course. We never let over the race
week. He also made an agreement with
me about board. I was to find for him
and the lady, and the servant, for 2*l.* 15*s.*
a week. That was without wine, beer,
or spirits. It is not a usual arrange-

ment.   We do it sometimes — not often.
The gentleman said it was because his
wife was not well, and could not be
troubled.   The servant was his.   It was
a maid.   She did not come with them.
The gentleman hired her at Brighton.
That is not a usual arrangement.   Certainly not.   I never made such a one
before, and I told him so.   He said it
was because he was so particular about
his servants.   He said he never would
live where the servants were not under
his own hand—where he could not turn
them away.   I said I did not like it—
it was not the custom.   He said he was
sorry, but he could not take the apartments without it, and then I gave way.
Afterwards he followed me down stairs,
and gave me to understand it was something about his wife.   At first, I thought
she was not quite right in her head.   That
was from what he told me.   I said I should
be afraid to have her in the house; but he
laughed, and said it was not that.   I then
supposed it must be temper.   He was very

pleasant about it.   He was always very
pleasant to me.   I don't know what he
may have been to other people.   I always
had my money to the day, and he was
always pleasant.   I can't say better
than that.   He got a servant a few days
after they came.   I did not turn away my
own.   I had none at the time.   The season
being over, it was a great chance whether
I let again, and I sent my servant away,
and did for myself.   A charwoman did for
the gentleman till he got a servant.   He
got one from Brighton.   I recommended
two or three in Bognor, but they did not
suit.   The one he got was a girl about
twenty.   Her name was Sarah something.
I did not think much of her.   I used sometimes to think my tea and sugar went very
fast.   I never caught her taking anything.
She was very quiet and civil-spoken.   She
stayed with the gentleman about a month;
not quite.   She was sent away for giving the
lady a dose of physic in her arrow-root to
make her sick.   The lady was very bad
indeed.   We thought she would have died.

She was dreadfully sick, and had the cholera
awfully bad.   This was the 9th of December.*   I know it from my books.   The
gentleman sent out for brandy and several
things, and they are down in my book.
On the following morning he sent for some
stuff from the chemist.†   Before that he
had given her some medicine himself.   I
don't know what it was.   He had a lot of
chemicals and things.   He kept them in a
back room.   The lady had a doctor.   Not
at first.   Not till the Monday after she
was ill.   I asked him to send for one, but
he said he was a doctor himself.   She continued very ill, and on the Sunday night
I asked him again.   He said, if she was not
better next morning, he would.   I wanted
him to send for Dr. Pesketh or Dr. Thompson, but he would not.   He said they were
no good.   I have always heard them very
highly spoken of.   Dr. Pesketh I have

* Compare Mrs. Anderton's Journal, December 9,
p. 80.

† On enquiry I find this to have been the decoction of Peruvian bark.—R. H.,

always heard of as a first-rate doctor. He
is since dead. Dr. Thompson is a very
good doctor, too; but Dr. Pesketh, perhaps, had most practice. I don't think
the gentleman knew anything about either
of them. He sent for a Dr. Jones, who
was in lodgings in the Steyne. I believe
he lived in London. He prescribed for
the lady while he stayed in Bognor. He
went away the week after. He was only
there a fortnight. The gentleman heard
of him through a friend of mine in the
Steyne. He asked me to find out whether
there was no London doctor in the place.
He would not have anyone that belonged
to the place. He said country doctors
were no good. The lady got better, but
very slowly. She was ill several weeks.
When she was strong enough, they went
away. He was very attentive to her.
Never left her alone for a minute hardly.
She did not seem very fond of him. I
think she was afraid of him, but I don't
know why. He was very kind to her,
and always particularly civil. Sometimes

she seemed quite put out like by his
civility. I thought sometimes she would
have flown out at him. She never did
fly out. He always seemed able to stop
her. I don't know how he did it. He
never said anything; only looked at her;
and it was quite enough. I thought she
must have been doing something wrong,
and he had brought her to Bognor to be
out of the way. I do not know exactly
what made me think so. It was the way
they went on, and what he said to me.
He never told me so. It was from things
he said. I did not talk much to the lady.
I thought her very ungrateful when he
was so kind. Then she was hardly ever
alone. Only once, when the gentleman
went out for something. Then she was
left about an hour. She was writing part
of the time. She borrowed writing ma-
terials of me. There were none in the
sitting-room. There usually were, but the
gentleman had sent the inkstand down-
stairs. He said it was sure to be upset.
I lent the lady the things, and she gave me

two letters for the post. She did not say anything to me ; only asked me to post them immediately. One was addressed to Notting Hill. I noticed that, because I have a sister living there; the other was to some theatre. I forget where. It struck me, because I thought it odd that a lady should write to a theatre. I didn't think it was right. I would rather not say what I thought. Well, it was that she was connected with some one there. Improperly, of course. The letter was not addressed to a man. It was " Miss Somebody," but that might be a blind. I thought this might account for her behaviour to her husband. I was very angry. A woman has no business to go on so. It is particularly bad when she has such a good husband. I did not say this to her. I did not notice the address till I got down-stairs. I kept the letters, and told the gentleman when he came in. He seemed very much vexed. He took the letters, and was very much obliged to me. He put the. letter to the theatre

into the fire without opening it.   The
other he said he would post himself.   I
don't know whether he did post it, or not.
I suppose so, of course.   I think he spoke
to the lady about it.   I am sure he did;
for, that night, when I went up, I could
see she had been crying, and she would
never speak to me again.   She spoke English quite well.   The letters were addressed
in English.   When she spoke to the gentleman it was generally in some foreign
language, but she could speak English perfectly.   I do not know what became of the
girl, Sarah.   I think she went into service
again at Brighton.   I know the gentleman
gave her a character.   He was very kind
to her.   He was always very kind.   He
was the pleasantest and most civil-spoken
gentleman I ever met, and I think his wife
behaved very bad to him.'

4. *Statement of Dr. Jones, of Gower Street,
Bedford Square.**

'I am a physician, residing in Gower
Street, Bedford Square.   In the beginning

* Compare Section III., 2.

I

of December 1854, I was suffering from a severe cold, and being unable to shake it off, went for a fortnight to the sea for change of air. I selected Bognor, because I had been in the habit of spending my holidays there for two or three years. I was lodging in the Steyne. Some few days after my arrival, I received a message requesting me to call and see a lady who was dangerously ill at a lodging in another part of the town. At first I declined to go, not wishing to interfere with the established practitioners of the place. A gentleman then called upon me, who gave the name of the Baron R**. He informed me that the lady in question was his wife, and that she was dangerously ill from the effects of a considerable quantity of emetic tartar, administered to her by the maid. He was very urgent with me to attend, saying that he was in the greatest anxiety about his wife, and that he could not in such a case sufficiently rely upon the skill of any country doctor. He pressed me so strongly, that I at length consented to accompany him to his lodgings. I found the patient in a very exhausted condition, and evidently suffering from the effects of some irritant poison. From what the Baron told me, the symptoms were much abated, but the disturbance still continued, accompanied with severe griping pains and profuse perspirations. I learned from the Baron that, being himself a good amateur chemist, and having accidently discovered at the outset the origin of his wife's illness, he had so far treated her himself, rather than trust to the chance of a country physician. He described his treatment, which appeared to me perfectly correct. On becoming satisfied of the cause of the disturbance, he first promoted vomiting as much as possible by the exhibition of tepid water, and afterwards of warm water, with a small quantity of mustard. When no more food appeared to be left in the stomach, he then administered large quantities of a saturated infusion of green tea, of which he had a few pounds at hand for his own drinking, and, finally, at the time of my arrival was exhibiting considerable doses of decoction of Peruvian bark: both which remedies are recommended by Professor Taylor in cases of antimonial poisoning. Their action left no doubt on my mind as to the origin of the symptoms; but by desire of the Baron I proceeded to make with him the customary analyses; carefully testing, also, a portion of the arrow-root in which the tartarised antimony was supposed to have been administered. In each case we together applied the usual tests,—viz., nitric acid, ferrocyanide of potassium, and hydrosulphuret of ammonia,—and succeeded in ascertaining beyond doubt the presence of antimony in all three. The quantity, however, appears to have been small. So far as we could ascertain, there could not have been more than one, or at the most two grains of tartarised antimony in the arrow-root, of which not much more than three parts was eaten. I cannot account for the violent action of so small a quantity. I have frequently administered much larger doses in cases of inflammation of the lungs without ill effect.   Two grains is by no means an unusual dose when intended to act as an emetic; but the action of anti-mony varies greatly with different consti-tutions.   Having certified ourselves of the presence of the suspected poison, the ques-tion was, as to the person by whom it had been administered.   The Baron said he had no doubt that it was a trick on the part of the servant maid, between whom and her mistress there had been some dispute a few days since.   We therefore determined on taxing her with it; but, before doing so, proceeded to examine a bottle of prepared tartar emetic, which, as the Baron informed me, he kept for his own use, being subject to digestive derangement.   He was, I be-lieve, addicted to the pleasures of the table, and was in the habit of taking an occasional emetic.   The bottle was not in its usual place, but was standing on the table at the side of the dressing-case in which it was usually kept.   It was labelled, " The emetic. One tea-spoonful to be taken as directed."

I remarked that it should be labelled "poison," and the Baron quite agreed with me, and immediately wrote the word in large characters on a piece of paper and gummed it round the bottle. We then weighed the contents of the bottle, from which three doses only had been taken by the Baron, and, on comparing the results, we found that a quantity equivalent to about one grain and a-half of the tartarised antimony had been abstracted in excess of this amount. The servant maid was the only person besides the Baron who usually had access to the apartment; and we at once sent for her and taxed her with having administered it to Madame R** in the arrow-root before mentioned. My own counsel was to give her immediately in charge, but the Baron pointed out, very justly, that there was nothing to show the girl that she was doing anything that could possibly affect life; and that, in the absence of any motive for such a crime, it was only fair to conclude that nothing was intended beyond a foolish practical joke. He said the same to the girl, and spoke to her very kindly indeed. At first she altogether denied it, and pretended to be quite astonished at such an imputation. The Baron, however, looked steadily at her and said, " Take care, Sarah! Remember what I said to you only three days ago." She did not attempt then to deny it any longer, but said she was very sorry, but she hoped the Baron would forgive her. The Baron said he could not possibly retain her in his service, and she then begged of him not to send her away without a character. At this time I interfered, and said he would be very wrong to send her into any other family after playing such a trick. She again protested she had meant no harm, and the subject then dropped, the Baron saying he would take time to consider of it. From that time I attended Madame R** until my return to London, when she was clearly recovering. I did not enter into any conversation with her, as she seemed very reserved and of an unsociable disposition. The Baron seemed an unusually attentive husband. Talking

over the subject of the seizure a day or
two afterwards, he informed me that the
death of his wife would also have been a
severe loss in a pecuniary point of view, as
if she lived she would inherit a considerable fortune.   I asked him why he did not
insure her life, and he said he should now
certainly do so, but had not before thought
of it.   He called upon me about two
months later, in passing through town, and
informed me that he intended to travel
abroad for some months.   I recommended
the German baths, and on his objecting to
the crowds of English there, suggested
Griesbach or Rippoldsau, in the Black
Forest, where Englishmen are rarely to be
encountered.   It was too early for either
place at that time, and I recommended the
south of France until the season was sufficiently advanced.   I did not see him again
till October 1855, when he again called
upon me with Madame R**, who seemed
perfectly restored, and of whom I had no
difficulty in reporting most favourably to
the ——— Life Assurance Association, as

also some weeks later to the —— Life
Office of Dublin, when applied to for my
professional opinion. I think Madame
R**'s was an excellent life, and there could
be no better proof of it than her entire recovery in the course of a very few months,
or indeed weeks, from so severe an illness.
The sensitiveness to antimony would not
affect this opinion. Indeed Professor Taylor, in his work on poisons, points out distinctly the "idiosyncratic" action of antimony and other medicinals on certain con-
stitutions, as "conferring on an ordinary
medicinal dose a poisonous instead of a
curative action." I have a copy of his
work now before me, in which he says that
" daily experience teaches us that some persons are more powerfully affected than
others by an ordinary dose of opium,
arsenic, *antimony*, and other substances ; "
and again, in considering the probable
amount of the "fatal dose," he speaks of
"that ever-varying condition of idiosyncracy, in which, as it is well known,
there is a state of constitution more liable

to be affected by antimonial compounds than other individuals apparently in the same conditions as to health, age," &c. I did not, therefore, nor do I now, consider the sensitiveness of Madame R**'s constitution to that medicine any objection to her life, especially in view of the immense vitality shown by her recovery. With regard to the sleep-walking, I have had no hint from the Baron of such a propensity on the part of Madame R**. Certainly it was never suggested that she could have poisoned herself in that way. Indeed, the servant girl admitted the act. The mode of Madame R**'s death does not in any degree shake my confidence in my former opinion, as such an occurrence might have happened, though by no means likely to do so, to any one in the habit of walking in their sleep, a propensity which in Madame R**'s case I had no means of ascertaining. I have been enabled to be thus precise in my statement, from the fact that the interesting nature of the case led me to make a special memorandum of it in my diary, from which the above is taken. I shall therefore have no difficulty in confirming any portion of it upon oath.'

5. *Statement of Mrs. Throgmorton.*

' MRS. THROGMORTON presents her compliments to Mr. R. Henderson, and begs to inform him that the girl, Sarah Newman, who is still in her service, and continues to give entire satisfaction in every way, came to her about Christmas, 1854, with a written character from the Baron R**, then residing at Bognor, and with whom she had been as housemaid and parlourmaid for some weeks. The character given by the Baron was a most satisfactory one, but on Mrs. Throgmorton's desiring to know the reason of Sarah Newman's leaving the situation, she was informed by the Baron that it was on account of her having played a foolish trick upon her late mistress by administering an emetic to her without authority, a highly reprehensible proceeding, which rendered Mrs. Throgmorton very much indisposed to receive her into her family. On further correspondence with Sarah Newman's late master, however, Mrs. Throgmorton received the impression that the fault had, in point of fact, been chiefly on the side of Madame R**, though, of course, as a gentleman, impossible to say so directly with respect to his own wife, and Mrs. Throgmorton therefore agreed to take Sarah Newman on trial, as she appeared truly penitent for her most reprehensible conduct, and has since proved a very valuable servant in every respect. Mrs. Throgmorton trusts that this information will be satisfactory to Mr. Henderson, as he appears interested in Sarah Newman's welfare, in whom Mrs. Throgmorton herself takes great interest.

' Cliftonville.'

6. *Statement of Mr. Andrews.*

' SIR,

' In reply to your letter of the 25th ult., I beg to inform you that the girl, Sarah Newman, certainly was in my service at Brighton for a month or two in the sum-

mer of 1854, but was discharged, I think,
in September, of that year, for various petty
thefts. She was a very interesting girl,
and took us in completely, but was accidently discovered by one of our children,
and after full proof of her delinquencies,
turned away without a character. My own
wish was to prosecute her, which indeed I
considered almost a duty to others by whom
she might hereafter be plundered; but I
was persuaded to relinquish my intention
by my wife, who had taken a great fancy
to her. About two months after her dismissal, a gentleman, who gave some German
name—I cannot now remember it—called
to enquire our reasons for discharging her,
and I then informed him of the whole case.
He questioned me pretty closely as to my
real opinion of the girl, stating that he was
philanthropically disposed, and would give
her a chance for reform, if there was any
likelihood of her availing herself of it. I
told him frankly my own opinion, viz., that
the girl was a hardened offender; but my
wife was very eager that she should have

another chance, and I have very little doubt
the German gentleman took her. He was, so
far as I remember, a stout good-natured
looking man, and he had with him a young
lady whom he left in the carriage, and who
was, he said, his wife. I think the name
you mention—Baron R**—is the same
name as that given—or at least something
like it—but cannot be quite sure.

' I am, dear Sir,

' Faithfully yours,

' CHARLES ANDREWS.

' P.S.—My wife begs me to ask that
should you know anything of the after-
career of her protégée, you will kindly
communicate it to us.

'R. Henderson, Esq., &c., &c., &c.,
  ' Clement's Inn, W.C.'

6, *Statement of Sarah Newman.*

N.B.—This statement was not obtained
without considerable difficulty, and must
be taken for whatever it may be worth.
The girl was naturally anxious to be secured against the possible consequences of

her own admissions, and I only at last succeeded in inducing her to speak out by
means both of a promise on the part of
Mrs. Throgmorton not to discharge her,
and a threat of police interference if she
did not confess the whole truth. I have,
myself, no doubt whatever of the correct-
ness of her statement as it now stands, and
it is, as you will see, corroborated in several
very important particulars; but whether it
could be produced before a jury, or, if it
were so, what effect it would have upon
their minds, are both very doubtful questions.   R. H.

Statement.

' My name is Sarah Newman. I was in
the service of Mr. Andrews, at Brighton,
for three months. I was discharged by him
for stealing tea and sugar. Mr. Andrews
wanted to take the law of me, but my mistress would not let him. My mistress
would have kept me on, but master said,
" No." She was always very kind to me,
and it was very ungrateful of me to rob her.
I would never do so again. My present

mistress is very kind to me, too. I have never robbed her of a pin. I declare to goodness I have not, nor I never will steal from anybody again. I have often wanted to tell Mrs. Andrews so since, but did not know where she was. I did not say it to her when I left. I felt quite hard like, because of master. I was out of place two months after that. No one would take me without a character. At last a friend at Bognor told me of a gentleman, and I got her to speak to him. It was the Baron. He came to see me one day when he was at Brighton. He insisted on knowing all about me— where I had been and why I had left Mr. Andrews. He was very kind, and said it was hard a poor girl should be ruined for one false step. He said if I would promise never to steal again he would give me a trial. I promised him faithfully, and he at last took me down to Bognor with him. I do not know whether he made any enquiries about me. I think not. He did not tell me he had. I meant to keep my promise. Indeed I did, and I did keep it,

'The Baron came back and caught me. ... He just shut the door close and walked straight up to me. I was so frightened I could not move.'

almost. I mean I only took one little thing, and I really did not think that was stealing. Nothing was ever locked up. The Baron always insisted on having the tea-chest and other things left open, in case he wanted some. I never took any. I might have taken a great deal, but I did not. I used to think sometimes things were left on purpose to tempt me, but of course that was fancy. Often there were coppers left about, but I never touched them. I did take one thing at last. I did not think that was stealing. It was only some orange-marmalade. I am very fond of sweet things. One day there was a pot of orange-marmalade. It was left on the table. It was after they had gone away from breakfast. I couldn't help it. It looked so nice. I just put in my finger. That was all. I declare to goodness that was all. I did not even taste it. The Baron came back and caught me. He did not say anything. He just shut the door close and walked straight up to me. I was so frightened I could not move. He took

K

hold of my wrist and held up my hand.   I
burst out crying.   He said it was no use
crying ; I had deceived him, and must
go.   He said if he did his duty he ought
to give me up to the police.   I said indeed
I had taken nothing, but only that little
taste of sweets.   He said, who would believe me with my character?   He spoke
very kind but very stern, and I was dreadfully frightened.   I begged of him not to
give me up, and he said he would give
me one chance more; but I must go
away.   I said, if he turned me out without a character, I might as well drown
myself at once.   I begged him to let me
stay; but he said that was impossible.
Then I begged him not to say why I
was sent away.   He said, what else could
he say?   I begged him again very hard.
At last he said he would think over it.
He said he would try and make some other
excuse for my going, but I must go next
day, positive.   He told me, if he did make
an excuse for me, to be very careful not to
contradict him.   I was very grateful to

him. He is a kind, good gentleman, and I
shall always bless him for it. I did not go
next day. I was kept by my mistress's illness. She was very bad indeed. I did all I
could for her. I hoped the Baron had forgotten and would let me stay. He sent for
me two or three days afterwards. There was
another gentleman with him. It was the
doctor. He charged me with having given
some stuff to my mistress to make her sick.
Of course I denied it. *I never gave her
anything.* I never had any quarrel with
her at all. She was always very good-
natured to me, but I did not like her much.
I don't know why. I think it was because
she did not like master. I said I had given
her nothing. No more I had. I never saw
the bottle, and don't know what it was. I
cannot read at all. I saw master look at
me, and he said something about two or
three days ago. I knew then that he was
making an excuse to send me away. He
made signs at me to abide by what he said,
and I did abide by it. The other gentleman was very hard, but of course he did

not know.   What the Baron said was given
as a reason for my going away.   That was
all.   The real reason was my taking the
marmalade.   If you ask the Baron, he will
tell you so.   I hope you will tell him how
grateful I am for his kindness to me.'

Section V.

1.—*Memorandum by Mr. Henderson.*

WE have now reached a point in this mysterious story at which I must again direct your attention most particularly to the coincidences of dates, &c., on which, indeed, depends entirely, as I have before said, the only solution at which I have found it possible to arrive.

The length to which these depositions have run has obliged me to divide them into distinct sections, each of which should bear more directly upon some particular phase of the case. For this purpose I have taken, as you will have perceived, first the early history of Mrs. Anderton, and as we may, I think, fairly assume, of Madame R** also; thus establishing, at the outset, the initiatory link of that chain of connection between these two extraordinary cases, which, inexplicable as either is in itself, will nevertheless, I cannot but imagine, each help to elucidate the other. The second division placed us in possession of the histories both of Mrs. Anderton and Madame R**, up to the point at which the thread of their singular destinies crossed ; showing also, how the Baron became aware of his wife's probable relationship to Mrs. Anderton, and of the benefit thereby accruing to her upon the death, without issue, of her sister and Mr. Anderton. The third section deals with the first illness of Madame R**, to the date and circumstances of which I felt it right to direct your most particular attention.

In the fourth division of the evidence we then reviewed the circumstances attending the fatal illness of Mrs. Anderton, which led to her husband's arrest on suspicion of murder, and finally to his suicide while awaiting investigation. A considerable portion of the evidence connected with this phase of the subject I have thought it best

to keep back for insertion in that division
of the case which bears more particularly
upon the conduct and death of Mr. Anderton, and which will follow that on which
we are now about to enter. The narrative,
therefore, of Mrs. Anderton's last illness
has been thus far confined to the mention
of it in the unfortunate lady's own diary,
with the note at its termination, in which
her husband records the fact of her decease.
With this, however, I have coupled an account, drawn partly from an earlier portion
of the same diary, and partly from the
statement of the medical man by whom she
was at the time attended, of a previous illness very similar in general character to
that by which she was finally carried off,
and apparently of an equally unaccountable description. The object with which
I have thus placed in juxta-position the
first attacks respectively of Madame R**
and Mrs. Anderton will probably be
sufficiently apparent. I have now to
direct your attention to a second illness
of Madame R**, occurring, under what I

cannot but feel to be most suspicious circumstances, but a very few months before her demise.

In proceeding with this portion of the case, the extreme importance attaching to a thorough and correct appreciation of the dates of the various occurrences will become more obvious at every step, and to them I must again request your utmost attention. I had at first proposed to submit to you in a tabular form the singular coincidences to which I allude; but, on reflection, such a course appeared objectionable, as tending to place too strongly before you a view of the subject with which I must confess myself thoroughly dissatisfied. I have, therefore, preferred leaving entirely to yourselves the comparison of the various dates, &c., limiting myself strictly to a verification of their accuracy. In many instances this has been no easy task, and more particularly in establishing satisfactorily the exact date (5th April, 1856), at which the symptoms of Madame R**'s second illness first appeared, wherein I have experienced a difficulty only compensated by the importance of the result.

I have, therefore, to request that the depositions here following may be carefully compared with the concluding portion of Mrs. Anderton's diary, and also with the statement of Dr. Dodsworth. In making this comparison you will notice, besides the points I have already referred to respecting dates, various discrepancies between facts as actually occurring and as represented to Mr. and Mrs. Anderton by the Baron. These I need not here particularise, as they will be sufficiently obvious on a perusal of the depositions themselves; but it is as well to draw your attention generally to them, as they seem to have a significant bearing upon other parts of the case.

I must request you also to bear in mind the relation in which the Baron and his wife were supposed to stand towards each other previously to their marriage, and will now proceed to lay before you the depositions relating, as I have said, to the second illness of the latter.

2.—*Statement of Mrs. Brown.*

' My name is Jane Brown. I am a widow, and my poor dear husband was a clerk in the city. I don't know in whose house. I did know, but I forget. My memory is very bad. I live in Russell Place. The house is my own, not hired. My poor dear husband left it to me in his will. I sometimes let it off in lodgings. Not always. Only when I can get quiet lodgers. Last year* I let the first and second floors to Baron R**. The ground-floor was let to Dr. Marsden. He has had it several years. He does not live there. He has a practice near London. He comes to Russell Place every Monday and Friday to see his patients. He used to live with us. That was in my poor dear husband's lifetime. Baron R** took the rest of the house, except the attics. I lived there myself. I cannot remember when the Baron came. It was some time in February or March. I am sure I cannot remember. I have no

* 1856.—R. H.

means of ascertaining. I don't keep any
accounts. My poor dear husband always
kept the accounts. I have kept none since
he died. I dare say I lose money by it,
but I can't help it. I have no head for it.
I am pretty sure it was in February or
March. I think about the beginning of
March.* There was no other lodger then.
Not till my son went away from home
again. He was away from home then. He
came home some time in March or April.
I suppose it was in March. He came from
Melbourne to Liverpool. He was at home
for some weeks. I can't tell how many.
He went away again in April, or it might
have been May. I am almost sure it was
not later than May. Not so late I think.
Mrs. Troubridge could tell you. Richard
married her daughter. Richard is my son.
He married Ellen Troubridge. That was
while he was at home last year. They had
been engaged ever so long. He came home
on purpose to marry her. He had got a

* Clearly so. The Baron was in Dublin on 25th
Feb.—R. H.

promise of something at Melbourne, and
was obliged to go back directly.   He
worked his passage home from Melbourne.
I do not know what ship he came in.   I
don't think he shipped in his own name.   I
forget why it was.   Something about not
liking to have it known.   I don't know
why not.   I don't know at all what name
he took.   I cannot remember when he came
home or when he went.   I do not know
when he left   Melbourne.   He brought
home one paper.   There is only a small
piece of it left.   He was with me all the
time he was at home, except Saturdays and
Sundays.   He used to go down to Brighton
then to see Ellen.   She was in a shop
there.   He used to go by the excursion
train and stay with her mother from Saturday to Monday.   All the rest of the time
he was with me.   That is all I can tell you
about him.   The other lodger was a friend
of his.   He had known him in Australia.
He asked him to his wedding.   That was at
our house.   It was on a Monday, and he
came the Saturday before.   They all came

up together from Brighton. The Baron
let us use his rooms. He went away somewhere to give his lady change of air. I
think it was because she had been ill. I
cannot be sure. She was ill several times
at my house. She died there. I forget
when was the first time she was ill there.
It was while my son was in England. I
remember talking to him about it. He was
away from home at the time. There was
no one in the house but myself. I remember it because I was so frightened.
There was nobody at all. Not even a
servant. I generally have a servant. I
was without one then for two or three
months. I got a charwoman to come in
the day. The reason was my servant got
tipsy. She had to be taken away by the
police, and I was afraid for a long while to
get another. I can't at all remember when
that was. I think it must have been before
the Baron came. I can't be sure. I am
quite sure it was before Madame R** was
taken ill. I am sure of that because I remember so well how frightened I was. I

think Dr. Marsden attended Madame R**.
He used to be very friendly with the Baron.
Everybody liked him. He was so good-
natured and so very kind to his wife. We
did not think so much of her. She was
very quiet, but she did not seem to care
about him. She seemed frightened like. I
sometimes thought she was not quite right
in her head. The Baron was always kind
to her. He was good-natured with everybody. I never heard him say a hard word
of anyone but once. That was of young
Aldridge. He was Richard's friend who
lodged with us.* He made a noise and disturbed Madame R**. He came in one night
quite intoxicated, and the Baron asked me
to give him notice. He said if Mr. Aldridge
did not go, he must. Of course I gave him
notice directly. He said it was all spite.
Of course I knew that was not true. He
said he was not drunk, but the policeman
found him lying on the doorstep. I forget

---

* This portion of Mrs. Brown's evidence affects
more particularly the part of the case to be hereafter
referred to in Part vii. ; but I have thought it best
to preserve it intact.—R. H.

*'He said he was not drunk, but the policeman
found him lying on the doorstep.'*

what he said. It was some foolish story about the Baron. I do not know of any reason why they should have quarrelled. I remember he said something once about Madame R** walking in her sleep. I don't know what it was. I don't think that could have had anything to do with it. Of course it could not. The Baron complained of being disturbed. That was all. I do not remember that I was ever disturbed myself. His room was next to mine. I might have been disturbed without remembering. I certainly was disturbed that night he came home intoxicated. He might have disturbed Madame R**, and I slept through it. I sleep heavy sometimes. I forget when this was and when he left the house. I cannot remember the exact dates of anything. My poor dear husband always did everything of that sort for me. He was a very exact man. I have no sort of books or papers of any kind to which I could refer. This is all I can tell you about it.'

3. *Statement of Mrs. Troubridge.*

'My name is Ellen Troubridge. My husband is a seafaring man. He is captain of a small collier. We live at Shoreham, near Brighton. I have one daughter, whose name is Ellen. She is married to a man of the name of Richard Brown. He is in Australia. He went out to Australia in 1856. I forget the exact date. It was some time in April or May. The ship's name was the Maria Somes. She sailed from Gravesend. My daughter was married on the 14th of April. That was not very long before they sailed. She had been engaged to young Brown for three or four years. He came home on purpose to marry her. I don't remember exactly when he came home. It must have been about a month before. Something of that kind. He was in a great hurry to get out again. He wanted to marry by license, so as to be quicker, but I told him it was a foolish expense. He had the banns put up the first Sunday he was at home. I think it was the first, but cannot be quite sure. My daughter was then in service. She was at a shop in Brighton. During the week she used to sleep at a friend's house, and on Saturdays she used to come home to us for Sundays. Brown used always to come down on Saturdays. He used to come by the cheap excursion train. He used to go to Brighton and call for Nelly, and walk with her to Shoreham. He used to walk back with her early Monday morning, and go on to town. He never came at other times. It was no good. Nelly was only at home Sundays. He wanted her to leave and go to his mother's. She would not leave the shop until her time was out. I would not let him be at Brighton. I was afraid people might talk. So far as I know, he was at home all the rest of the time. The marriage took place from Mrs. Brown's house. She had a lodger then—a foreigner, I think. He went out of town for two or three days, and lent her his rooms. After the wedding, young Brown and my daughter went to Southend for a few days. I cannot say exactly how long. About a week or a fortnight. On the Saturday before they sailed, we all went down to Gravesend to meet them and see them off. The ship was to have sailed on the Sunday. We all went to Rosherville, and slept at Gravesend that night. I had some friends there, who gave us beds. Mrs. Brown went back on Sunday, but I stayed. A young man by the name of Aldridge was with us. He was a friend of Brown's. I did not much like him. He went back with Mrs. Brown. I think he took lodgings in her house. I cannot call to mind the exact day young Brown came home. I think it must have been some time in March.'

4. *Statement of Dr. Marsden.*

'My name is Anthony Marsden. I am a physician, and formerly resided at Mrs. Brown's house, in Russell Place. Some three or four years ago I found the atmosphere of London beginning to tell upon my health, and determined to remove into the

suburbs.   I bought a small practice in the
neighbourhood of St. John's Wood, and
gave up the greater portion of my London
patients.   I was, however, desirous of not
altogether relinquishing that connection,
and with this object rented two rooms at
Mrs. Brown's, where I might be consulted
by such patients as I still retained in that
neighbourhood.   I used to drive up for
this purpose every Monday and Friday
morning.   I had been doing this for some
time, when the first and second floor apartments were taken by the Baron R**.   I
did not at first much like him.   I thought
him an impostor.   He seemed, however, to
wish to make my acquaintance, and I found
that he was, at all events, a very highly
informed man on all matters of science.
We had frequent conversations respecting
mesmerism.   He certainly seemed to be
himself a believer in it.   Were I not myself thoroughly satisfied of its impossibility,
I am not at all sure but that he might have
convinced me on the subject.   I am quite
unable to account for many of the pheno-

mena exhibited. They were, however, of course to be accounted for in some way. He seemed a very excellent chemist, and we used at times to pursue our investigations together. There was a small room at the back of the house, on the basement floor, which he used as a laboratory. He invited me to make use of it, and I was frequently there. He was always engaged in experiments of one kind or another, and had various ingenious projects in hand. In the laboratory was a large assortment of chemicals and medicines of various kinds. In the case of poor patients, I have sometimes asked him to make up a prescription, and he has done so. At the time at which I knew him, he was engaged in a series of experiments on the metals, and more especially on mercury, antimony, lead, and zinc. I think he must have had almost every preparation of these that is made. I believe that his researches were for the purpose of finding a specific against the disease so prevalent among painters, which is known by the name of 'lead colic.' The laboratory was at the back of the house, and quite detached from all the other rooms. There was an open space between it and the rest of the house, with only a passage communicating with the offices. This pas-sage was shut off by a glass door, and there was a wooden door at the end into the laboratory. Both these doors were always kept closed. They were not usually locked. I told the Baron I thought they should be, but he said no one would go there. He had a weight put on to the laboratory door to close it. The glass door had a spring already. I frequently made use of his laboratory: sometimes when he was absent. I might go there with or without him, whenever I pleased. There was no attempt at concealing from me anything whatever that was done there. It was all quite open. I attended Madame R** through greater part of her illness. It was a very long affair, and of a very singular character. I cannot be at all certain as to the date at which it commenced. I was not regularly called in at the time, and did not notice it in my book. The Baron only consulted me in a friendly way about it, two or three days afterwards. It was certainly as much as that. I think it was the third day. I cannot be sure of that, but I am quite sure it was at least the second. By being the second day, I mean that at least one clear day had intervened between the night on which she was ill and the day on which I was consulted by the Baron. I cannot swear to more than one, but I think it must have been. From what the Baron told me of the symptoms, I remember concluding it to be a case of English cholera, but she was almost recovered at the time I first heard of it, and I did not prescribe for her. About a fortnight or three weeks after this she had another slight attack, for which the Baron himself also prescribed. He acquainted me on my visit to town with the course he had pursued, and I entirely concurred in his treatment of the case. The attack, however, returned I think more than once, and he then asked me to see and prescribe for her. I first saw her professionally on

the 23rd of May, 1856.* This was two
days after the third or fourth attack, which
occurred on the night of the 21st of May.
As soon as I regularly took up her case, I
made notes of it in my diary. Extracts
from this are enclosed (*vide* 5 *herewith*),
showing the progress of the case from time
to time. I attended her throughout her
illness. The attacks occurred, as will be
seen from my diary, about every fortnight.
They increased in intensity up to the 10th
of October, 1856. At this time, she was
apparently, for three or four days, almost
'in articulo mortis,' and I was unable to
hold out any hope of her recovery. Another
attack would certainly have been fatal.
Happily the disease appeared to have spent
itself, and at the expiration of the fortnight
no renewal of the more acute symptoms was
experienced. From this date, Madame R**
progressed slowly but steadily to convalescence, and would no doubt have ultimately
entirely recovered, but for the unfortunate ac-

* Comp. Journal of Mrs. Anderton, 25th May and
10th June: *Vide* Section III., 3.

cident which put an end to her life. Madame
R**'s case was one of great difficulty. It
was apparently one of chronic 'gastritis;'
but its recurrence in an acute form at stated
intervals was a very abnormal incident.
The case presented, in fact, all the more
prominent features of that of chronic antimonial poisoning recorded by Dr. Mayerhofer in "Heller's Archiv., 1846," and
alluded to by Professor Taylor in his work
on "Poisons," p. 539., There were also
strong points of general resemblance to the
other cases of M'Mullen and Hardman,
quoted by Professor Taylor at the same
page, and recorded in Guy's Hospital Re-
ports for October 1857. As matters progressed, I took the opportunity of pointing
this out as delicately as I could to the
Baron, and asked if he had any suspicions
of foul play. He seemed at first almost
amused by the suggestion; but upon further consultation was inclined to take a
graver view of the matter. We went carefully through the cases in question, the
Baron translating that of Dr. Mayerhofer

for my benefit, as I was not a German
scholar. At his suggestion, we determined
to make the customary analyses, and an
examination was accordingly instituted in
the Baron's laboratory. He was always
very particular in keeping up the supply
of medicine, and would never allow the
bottles, &c., to be thrown away. There
was therefore some remnant of every medicine that had been made up for her. These,
with the other subjects of analysis, we
tested carefully, both for arsenic and for
antimony, but without finding the slightest
trace of either. The analysis was conducted
by the Baron, who took the greatest interest
in it. I could not perhaps have done it
myself. Such matters have not come within my line of practice. In such a case I
should certainly not trust to my own
manipulations. I trusted to those of the
Baron, because I knew him to be an expert
practical chemist, and in the daily habit of
such operations. My own share in them
was limited to the observation of results,
and their comparison with those pointed out

by Professor Taylor. I did not take any
special pains to ascertain the purity of the
chemical tests employed or of their being
in fact what they were assumed to be.
That is to say, when a colourless liquid,
with all the apparent characteristics of
nitric acid was taken from a bottle labelled
" Nit. Ac.," I took for granted that nitric
acid was being employed. Similarly, of
course, with the other chemical agents. It
never occurred to me to do otherwise. Nor
did I take any especial precautions to
identify the matters examined. Others
might certainly have been substituted; but
if so, it must have been done by the Baron
himself. It was, perhaps, possible that he
might have conducted his investigations,
under such supervision as I then exercised,
with fictitious tests, and it was quite so to
substitute other matters and mislead me by
subjecting them to a real analysis. That
is to say, this would have been possible to
be done by the Baron. No one else could,
under the circumstances, have done it, or
at least without his direct connivance. I

had no ground for any suspicion of the kind, nor do I see any now. I think it most unwarrantable. Every circumstance that came under my notice goes equally to contravene such a supposition. The Baron was devotedly attached to his wife; he supplied her liberally with professional advice, as also with nurses, medicine, and every necessary; his care for her led him to precautions which, in their incidental results, must have inevitably exposed any attempt at the administration of poison. During the severer period of the disorder, he had no opportunity of attempting such a crime, as he universally insisted on both food and medicine being both prepared and administered by the nurses; he himself rendered every assistance in the endeavour to detect any such attempt when its possibility had been suggested by myself; and lastly, Madame R** did not die, although the investigation had already removed all suspicion. I think such an imputation wholly unwarranted and unwarrantable from any one circumstance of the case.'

5. *Extracts from Dr. Marsden's Diary.**

May 23rd.—Madame R**, nausea, sickness, tendency to diarrhœa, profuse perspiration, and general debility. Pulse low, 100. Spirits depressed. Burning pain in stomach — abdomen tender on pressure. Tongue discoloured.

26th.— Madame R** slightly better— less nausea and pain.

30th. — Madame R**. Improvement continues.

June 2nd.—Madame R** improving.

6th.—Ditto.

9th.—Recurrence of symptoms on Saturday evening.† Increased nausea, vomited matter yellow, with bile. Pulse low, 105.

---

* These extracts will, of course, be chiefly interesting to the medical profession, and may be passed over by the general reader. Some details are necessarily excluded. The notes, also, relating to the treatment adopted by Dr. Marsden, not materially affecting the question at issue, which is concerned only with the symptoms of disorder, are omitted as irrelevant, and therefore confusing. *Vide* note to statement of Dr. Watson, Section III., 2.

† 7th June.—R. H.

Throat sore, and slight constriction. Tongue foul.

13*th*.—Symptoms slightly ameliorated. Treatment continued.

16*th*.—Ditto.   Tongue slightly clearer. Pulse 100.

20*th*.—Improvement continued.   Pulse slightly firmer.

23*rd*.—Ditto.

24*th*.—Special visit.   Return of symptoms last night.   Great increase of nausea and vomiting — very yellow with bile. Throat sore and tongue foul.   Abdomen very tender on pressure.   Slight diarrhœa. Tingling sensation in limbs.

27*th*.—Slight improvement.

30*th*.—Continued, but slight. Pulse firmer.

July 3*rd*. — Improvement continued, especially in throat.   Perspiration still distressing.   Less tingling in limbs.

6*th*. — Improvement continued.   Pulse somewhat firmer, 110.

(10*th* to 20*th*.—Absent in Gloucestershire.)

20*th*.—A slight rally.   Baron says, attack

shortly after last visit, but recovery for time more rapid.

24th.—Improvement continues, but less rapid. Pulse 110.

27th.—Recurrence yesterday. General symptoms as before, much aggravated. Soreness and aphthous state of mouth and throat. Perspiration. Pain in abdomen. Complains of taste in mouth like lead. Pulse low, 115. Qy. antimony? Speak, Baron.

31st.— Analysis—satisfactory. Symptoms slightly abated.

August 3rd. — Improvement continued. Pulse 112, firmer.

7th.—Same.

10th.—Return of sickness, &c. General aggravation of symptoms. Patient much prostrated.

24th, 28th, 31st.—Slight improvement.

September 4th.—Improvement continued, but slight.

7th.—Return of severe symptoms. Vomiting, extremely yellow, much bile. Diarrhœa. Pulse low and fluttering, 120. Violent perspiration. Slight wandering.

Extreme soreness and constriction of throat. Slight convulsive twitchings in limbs. Great exhaustion and prostration.

10*th*, 14*th*, 18*th*.—Very slight abatement of symptoms.

21*st*.—Violence of symptoms increased. Pulse 125. Great prostration.

25*th*, 28*th*. — Very slight amelioration. Pulse 125. Wandering.

October 1*st*, 4*th*, 8*th*.—Symptoms slightly less severe.

11*th*. — Aggravation of all symptoms. Pulse 132, low and fluttering. Face flushed and pale. Much convulsive twitching in limbs. Power of speech quite gone. Entire prostration. Can hardly live through night.

12*th*, 13*th*, 14*th*.—Special visits. No perceptible change.

15*th*.—Pulse a shade firmer, 136.

N.B.—From this date, recovery slow, but steady.

6. *Memorandum by Mr. Henderson.*

From the very vague nature of the foregoing evidence, so far as dates are concerned, it was, as you will at once perceive, no very easy task to determine the precise day of Madame R**'s first attack. To the view of the case, however, which I was even then inclined to adopt, this was a matter of the last importance, and I determined to spare no effort to elucidate it if possible from the very loose data furnished by the depositions. In this I have, I think, been successful; but as the process has been somewhat complicated, I must ask you to follow me through it step by step.

The difficulty of tracing the truth seemed at first sight not a little augmented by the fact that no one had been in the house but Mrs. Brown herself, whose memory, even had it afforded any clue, could not have been relied on. On further consideration, however, I began to fancy myself mistaken in this respect, and finally conceived a hope that this very fact might, if properly handled, prove an assistance instead of an obstacle to my investigation. The following was the course of reasoning I pursued.

There are only two points on which Mrs.

Brown appears to be certain; her son's presence in England, and her being herself alone in the house on the actual day in question. The only chances of success therefore seemed to be:—First, in ascertaining precisely the limit of time within which such a combination was possible; and, second, in determining by a process of elimination the actual day or days on which such a combination could fall.

The result has been far more complete than at the outset of the investigation I could venture to hope.

1st. For the period of time to which our researches should be directed.

This was obviously limited by the residence of Richard Brown in England, and my first efforts were therefore directed towards determining the exact dates of his arrival and departure.

1. On enquiry at Liverpool, I found that the only vessels which had arrived from Melbourne during the month of March 1856, were as follows:—

Ship.	Captain.	Owners.	Arrived.
James Baines	M'Donald	Jas. Baines & Co.	4th March
Lightning .	Enright .	„	24th „
Emma .	. Underwood.	Pilkington Bros.	27th „

Of these, the James Baines left Melbourne
on the 28th November, and the Lightning
on the 28th December. The exact date of
sailing of the Emma I have not been able
to ascertain, but it is immaterial to the case.

. The fragment of newspaper preserved
by Mrs. Brown has no date, nor could I at
first find any clue by which it might be
determined. The last paragraph, however,
commences as follows:—

SEASONABLE WEATHER !—The thermometer has, for
the last four days, never been lower than ninety
degrees in the shade. We wonder what our friends
in England would say to singing their Ch . . .
rols in such a . . . .

The remainder is torn off, but the mis-
sing syllables are clearly *Christmas Carols*,
and this shows clearly that the paper must
have been published after the departure of
the James Baines on the 28th November.
Richard Brown must, therefore, have come
home either in the Lightning or the Emma,

the earliest of which reached Liverpool on the evening of the 24th March. The 25th of March, therefore, is the earliest date from which our examination need commence.

2. From Mrs. Troubridge, mother of the young woman to whom Richard Brown was married during his stay in England, I learned that the young couple sailed for Sydney in the Maria Somes. Mrs. Brown was unable to give me the date of this vessel's departure, but a search through the file of the Times for April 1856, shows that she left Gravesend on the 23rd of that month. The period to be analysed is therefore confined to the interval between the 25th March and the 25th April, 1856.

3. During this period, as we learn from Mrs. Brown's statement, Richard Brown was at home every day except Saturdays and Sundays. These were respectively, 29th and 30th of March, and 5th, 6th, 12th, 13th, 19th, and 20th of April.

4. Dr. Marsden, in his evidence, states most distinctly that he did not see Madame R** until at least 'one clear day' had

elapsed after her attack. Dr. Marsden's visits take place on the Monday and Friday of each week. Madame R**'s seizure, therefore, did not occur on a Sunday. This reduces the days on which it may have happened to the 29th March, and 5th, 12th, and 19th April.

5. From Mrs. Troubridge's evidence we learn that Mrs. Brown and the whole party slept at Gravesend on the Saturday night previous to the sailing of the Maria Somes. Mrs. Brown was therefore absent from town on the 19th April. The issue is thus narrowed to the 29th March and the 5th and 12th April.

6. From Mrs. Brown's statement we learn that on the Saturday and Sunday preceding the wedding, her son's friend, Aldridge, slept at the house. The wedding took place on the 14th April. On the 12th April, therefore, Mrs. Brown was not alone. The only days, therefore, on which the occurrence, as described, could have taken place are the 29th March and 5th April.

At this point I feared for some time that my clue was at an end. This would, however, have been most unsatisfactory, as the possible error of a week in point of date would have seriously detracted from the trustworthiness of the entire case. The only possible chance of determining the point seemed to lie in ascertaining the precise date of the servant's dismissal, and it at length occurred to me that this might be accomplished by means of the police records of the Court before which she was carried. From them I found—

7. That the offence for which she was discharged was committed on Sunday, the 30th of March. On the 29th, therefore, she was still in Mrs. Brown's house. The only day, therefore, on which Madame R**'s first seizure could have taken place, as stated during Richard Brown's stay in England, and on a night when Mrs. Brown was alone in the house, was the 5th of April.

The importance of this date, thus fixed, you will, I think, at once perceive.

SECTION VI.

1. *Memorandum by Mr. Henderson.*

WE have now arrived at a point in this
extraordinary case at which I must again
direct your attention to the will of the late
Mr. Wilson. By this will, 25,000*l*. was, as
we have seen, bequeathed to Miss Boleton
(afterwards Mrs. Anderton), with a life
interest, after her death, to her husband.
At his decease, and failing children by his
marriage with Miss Boleton, the money
passed to the second sister, whom, as I have
before said, we may, I think, be justified
in identifying with the late Madame R**.
It seems, at all events, clear, both from the
circumstances attending the marriage of
the Baron, and from the observation made
by him at Bognor to Dr. Jones relative
to the pecuniary loss he would have sus-

tained by the death of his wife, that the
Baron himself believed and was prepared
to maintain this relationship, and that the
various policies of assurance effected on the
life of Madame R**—to the gross amount
of 25,000*l.*, the exact sum in question,—
were intended to cover any risk of her
death before that of her sister. This is all
that we need at present require. What
import should be attached to the degree of
mystery with which the whole affair, both
of the marriage and of the assurance, seems
to have been so carefully surrounded, will,
of course, be matter for consideration when
reviewing the whole circumstances of the
case. It is enough for our present purpose
that the Baron clearly looked upon his wife
as the sister of Mrs. Anderton, and calculated upon participation, through her, in
the legacy of Mr. Wilson. The lives of Mr.
and Mrs. Anderton thus alone intervened
between this legacy and the Baron's family,
and we have thus established, on his part,
a direct interest in their decease.

On the death of Mrs. Anderton, under

the circumstances detailed in an earlier portion of the case, the life of her husband only now stood in the way of Baron R**'s succession, and it is important to bear this in mind in considering, as we are now about to do, the various circumstances attendant on the death of that gentleman.

The chain of evidence on which hangs, as I have so often said, the sole hypothesis by which I can account for the mysterious occurrences that form the subject of our enquiry, is not only of a purely circumstantial character, but also of a nature at once so delicate and so complicated that the failure of a single link would render the remainder altogether worthless. Unless the case can be made to stand out clearly, step by step, in all its details, from the commencement to the end, its isolated portions become at once a mere chaos of coincidences, singular indeed in many respects, but not necessarily involving any considerable element of suspicion. It is for this reason that I have, as before stated, endeavoured to lay before you in a distinct and separate

form each particular portion of the subject.
Hitherto our attention has been entirely oc-
cupied with the death of Mrs. Anderton, the
coincident illness of Madame R**, and other
circumstances, the bearing of which upon
those occurrences will be more clearly shown
hereafter. We have now to consider the very
singular circumstances attending the lapse
of the second life—that of Mr. Anderton—
intervening, as we have seen, between Mr.
Wilson's legacy and Madame R**.

For the purpose of this enquiry, I propose
adducing pretty much the same evidence
as that given at the inquests held on the
bodies of Mrs. and Mr. Anderton. The final
result of the former of these inquests was,
as you are aware, a verdict of ' Died from
natural causes,' though the case was at first
adjourned for a fortnight, in order to admit
of a more searching examination of the
body, during which time Mr. Anderton remained in custody in his own house. In
the latter case the jury, after some hesitation, returned a verdict of ' Temporary in
sanity, brought on by extreme distress of

mind at the death of his wife, and suspicions respecting it which subsequently proved to have been unfounded.'   Our present concern, however, being with the conduct of the Baron rather than with that of Mr. Anderton, I have omitted portions not directly bearing upon this part in the matter, and have endeavoured to procure such additions to the evidence of Doctor Dodsworth and others as might serve to further elucidate the subject of our enquiry. I now, therefore, lay before you this portion of the case, with special reference to its bearing upon the proceedings of Baron R**.

2. *Doctor Dodsworth's Statement.*

'I was in attendance on the late Mrs. Anderton during the illness which terminated fatally on the 12th of October, 1856. I was first sent for by Mr. Anderton, on the night of the 5th of April* in that year. I found her suffering apparently from a slight attack of English cholera, but was

* Compare Section III., 3 &c.

unable to ascertain any cause to which it might be attributed.   There was nothing to lead to any suspicion of poisoning: indeed, this seemed to be rendered almost impossible by the length of time that had elapsed since the last time of taking food and that at which the attack commenced. This was at least three or four hours; whereas, had the symptoms arisen from the action of any poisonous substance, they would have shown themselves much earlier. This is only my impression from after consideration.   No idea of poison occurred to me at the time, nor should I now entertain any were I called in to a similar case.   I prescribed the usual remedies for the complaint under which I supposed Mrs. Anderton to be suffering.   They appeared to have their effect, though not so rapidly as I should have expected.   The symptoms appeared rather to wear themselves out.   I visited her several times, as the debility which ensued seemed greater than, under ordinary circumstances, should have followed on such an attack.   About a fort-

night later she had a fresh seizure, of a
very similar kind. This time, however,
the symptoms were aggravated, and accompanied by others of a more alarming
character. Of these the most conspicuous
were nausea, vomiting, violent perspiration,
and increasing tendency to diarrhœa. The
patient also complained of great sinking of
the heart, and of a terrible lowness of spirits,
almost amounting to a conviction that death
was at hand. In the course of another
fortnight or three weeks there was a fresh
recurrence of the symptoms. The tongue,
which in the former attacks had been
clammy and dry, was now covered thickly
with dirty mucus, and there was a greatly
increased flow of saliva. The condition of
the tongue became greatly aggravated as the
disease progressed, the mouth and throat
becoming ultimately very sore, with great
constriction of the latter. The abdomen
was distended, and very tender to the
touch, the liver also being very full and
tender. Pulse low and rapid, decreasing
in fulness as the disease progressed, and

reaching finally to 130 or 140; and the depression of spirits and sinking at the heart considerably increased.   The patient appeared to be daily losing strength, and at each attack, which seemed to return periodically at intervals of about a fortnight, the same symptoms appeared more severely than before.   Mr. Anderton seemed to be in the deepest distress.   From the time when the symptoms first became serious, he hardly ever left her side, administering both food and medicine with his own hand. So far as I am aware, Mrs. Anderton took nothing of any kind from any other person throughout the greater portion of her illness.   I have heard her say this herself, in his presence, shortly before her death.   For the last few weeks she took scarcely any nourishment, and could with difficulty swallow her medicine. The principal cause of this difficulty lay in the extreme nausea which followed any attempt to swallow, but it was greatly increased by the painful and constricted state of the throat, which was extremely rough and raw, and

rendered swallowing very painful. As
the disease progressed, the vomited matter became strongly coloured with bile,
and was of a strong yellow colour. The
oppression on the heart also increased,
until at length respiration was almost im-
peded. The heart and pulses also gradu-
ally lost power, and latterly the lower
portion of the body was almost paralysed,
the limbs being stiff, and the whole frame,
from the waist downward, very heavy and
cold. The patient also suffered from
severe cold perspirations, as well as from
heat and irritation of the upper portion
of the body, and from entire inability to
sleep. A very remarkable feature in the
case was, that notwithstanding this general sleeplessness, each fresh attack of the
malady was *preceded by a sound slumber*
of some hours' duration, from which she
appeared to be aroused by the return of
the more active symptoms of the disorder.
I tried all the usual remedies indicated
by such symptoms, but without any per-
manent effect; and I was a good deal

perplexed by the anomalous appearance of the case, and especially by its intermittent character, the symptoms recurring, as I have said, with increased severity, at regular intervals of about a fortnight. I mentioned my difficulty to Mr. Anderton, and asked if he would wish further advice. At his urgent request I consented, though with some hesitation, to meet Baron R**, who holds, as I was given to understand, a regular diploma from several of the foreign Universities, but whose practice has been of a somewhat irregular character. I first consulted with him on the 12th July.'*

[Dr. Dodsworth here details at some length how he became convinced of the Baron's great skill and knowledge of chemistry, and was finally persuaded to meet him in consultation.]

' After examination of the patient, however, and some conversation as to the nature of the symptoms and of the reme-

* Vide Section V., 5.

dies employed, I had some difficulty in
drawing from him (the Baron) any expression of opinion. He appeared, however, to agree entirely in the course hitherto pursued, and after some further conversation we separated. The consultation
took place in Mrs. Anderton's dressing-
room, and in passing by the wash-hand
stand on his way out, the Baron suddenly
took up a small bottle which was standing
there, and turning sharply upon me,
asked "If I had tried that?" On taking
it from his hand, I found it contained
tincture of tannin, a preparation much
used for the teeth. I was somewhat
startled by the suddenness of the question,
and replied in the negative, on which the
subject dropped. On my way home, however, I was again struck by the peculiarity of the Baron's manner in putting
the question; and on thinking the matter
over, the idea suddenly flashed across me
that tannic acid was the antidote to antimony, and that the symptoms of poisoning
by tartarised antimony, to which attention

had just been drawn by Professor Taylor,
in the case of the Rugely murder, closely
resembled in many respects those under
which Mrs. Anderton was then suffering.
At the first moment this supposition seemed
to account for all the mysterious part of
the case; but on reflection the difficulty
returned, for it seemed impossible that
the poison could have been administered
by any one but Mr. Anderton himself, and
I felt it still more impossible to suspect
him of such an act, in face of the evident
and extreme affection existing between
them.   On mature reflection, however, I
determined on trying, at all events for a
time, the course suggested by the Baron,
and accordingly exhibited large doses of
Peruvian bark, together with other medicines of the same kind. My suspicions were
at first increased by the improvement apparently effected by these remedies, and I
took occasion to ask Mr. Anderton, in a
casual way, in presence of the nurse and
one of the servants, whether he had any
emetic tartar or antimonial wine in the

house.   The manner of his reply entirely
removed from my mind any idea that either
of those present, at least, had any knowledge
of such an attempt as seemed implied by
the Baron, and on seeing that gentleman a
day or two after, I questioned him as to the
true bearing of his suggestion. He disclaimed,
however, any such meaning as I had been
disposed to attribute to his words, stating,
in a general way, that he had before known
great benefit to accrue from the exhibition
of such medicines in similar cases, and ex-
pressing a hope that they might be successful in the present instance.   Something,
however, in his manner, and especially the
great stress laid upon careful watching of
the patient's diet while under this course of
treatment, led me still to fancy that he was
not so entirely without doubt as he wished
me to believe; but that, on the contrary,
his suspicions pointed towards Mr. Anderton, his friendship for whom made him
desirous of concealing them.   This opinion
was confirmed by the recollection of another
apparent instance of suspicion on the part

of the Baron, to which, a few days previously, however, I had not at the time
attached any importance. I accordingly
continued the bark treatment, determining,
should any fresh attack occur, to take measures for investigating the matter; for
which purpose I gave private orders to
the nurse, on whom I knew that I could
thoroughly depend, to allow nothing to be
removed from the room until I had myself
seen the patient. The beneficial effects of
the bark continued for about ten or twelve
days, at the end of which period I was sent
for hurriedly in the middle of the night, the
disease having returned with greater violence than at any previous attack. Having
done what was in my power to alleviate
the immediate pressure of the symptoms, I
took an opportunity of securing portions of
such matters as are tested in suspicious
cases, which I immediately had submitted to
a searching chemical analysis. No trace,
however, of antimony, arsenic, or any similar
poison, could be detected, and as the tannic
acid appeared now to have lost its remedial

power, I came finally to the conclusion that
its apparent efficacy had been due to some
other unknown cause, and that the suspicions of the Baron were altogether without
foundation. I continued the former treatment, varied from time to time as experience
suggested, but without being able to arrest
the progress of the disease, which I am inclined to think must have been constitutional
in its character, and probably hereditary, as I
learned from Mr. Anderton that the patient's
mother had been subject to some internal
disease, the exact symptoms of which, however, he was unable to call to mind. Towards the close of the case the patient was
almost constantly delirious from debility,
and the immediate cause of death was entire
prostration and exhaustion of the system.
I wished Mr. Anderton to allow a post-
mortem examination, with a view to dis-
covering the true nature of the disorder,
but he seemed so extremely sensitive on
the subject, and was in such a state of
nervous depression, that I forbore to press
the point. The Baron also seemed to dis-

courage him from such an idea. Subsequently an order came for an inquest, and I then assisted at the analysis which followed, and which was performed by Mr. Prendergast. We found no traces of antimony in any part of the body or its contents. The report of Mr. Prendergast, in which I fully concurred, will show the result of the analysis. Looking at that, and at all the circumstances of the case, I was, and still am, convinced that Mr. Anderton was perfectly innocent of the crime imputed.'

In answer to the queries forwarded at various times by Mr. Henderson, Dr. Dodsworth gives the following replies:—

' 1. In questioning the Baron as to his suggestion respecting the tincture of tannin, I put it plainly to him whether he had been led to make it by any suspicion of poison. This he disclaimed with equal directness, but with such hesitation as convinced me that the suspicion was really in his mind.

' 2. I told the Baron that I had exhibited bark and other similar remedies, and with

what success. He smiled, and turned the
conversation.

‘3. The Baron was not present at the
post-mortem examination. He wished very
much to be so, but Mr. Prendergast objected so strongly that I was obliged to
refuse him. I promised, however, to let
him know by telegraph the result of the
examination, which took place at Birming-
ham, where Mr. Prendergast was living at
the time. I enclose a copy of the message
sent. He offered to assist in removing the
intestines, &c., from the body, but this I
also declined, as Mr. Prendergast had particularly requested me to allow no one to
come near the body after it was opened but
myself and some student or surgeon from
one of the great hospitals, to render such
assistance as might be necessary. The
caution was, I think, a very reasonable
one, and I followed it out strictly.

‘4. The Baron certainly seemed at first,
as I thought, annoyed at being excluded,
but I attributed this to his interest in the
case. He did not make the request as to

telegraphing at the time, but wrote to me afterwards on the subject.

'5. The object of Mr. Prendergast's precaution was, of course, to prevent the body from being tampered with.

'6. By tampered with, I mean in such manner as to destroy the traces of the poison.

'7. It would, of course, be possible to manufacture traces of poison where none had previously existed; but this could only be done with the view of fastening on an innocent person the guilt of a murder which had never been committed, and was by no means what we intended to guard against in the exclusion of his friends.

'8. Certainly, had such a thing been successfully attempted in this instance, it would have rendered the case almost conclusive against Mr. Anderton.

'9. The other incident to which I have alluded, as evincing suspicion on the part of the Baron, was as follows:—We were one morning in consultation in Mr. Anderton's room. I wished to seal a letter. The

Baron lighted a taper for me with a piece of paper which he took from the waste basket. As he did so, he appeared struck with something on the paper, and untwisted it and showed it to me. There were only a few letters on it, part having been torn off and part burned. The letters were . . . RTAR EME . . . and part of what was evidently a T. Beneath was the upper portion of a capital P in writing. I did not, however, take much notice of it, and the thing passed from my mind.

' 10. I have no doubt myself that the paper came from the waste basket. The Baron said so. I did not actually see him take it out, but I saw him stoop to do so. There was nothing physically impossible in his having taken the paper from his own pocket, but I cannot see the slightest reason for such a supposition. The only object he could possibly have had in such an act would have been that of throwing suspicion on Mr. Anderton, and his whole desire evidently was to conceal the suspicions in his own mind as far as possible.

'11. The Baron gave me no other grounds for supposing that he suspected anything. On the contrary, he was continually pointing out to me the affection of Mr. Anderton for his wife, and especially the assiduity of his attendance in permitting no one else to administer either food or medicine.

'12. The practical effect of all this was certainly, I admit, to impress upon my own mind the suspicious circumstances of the case more strongly perhaps than if they had been pointed out in a directly hostile manner. It is impossible, however, that the Baron could have reckoned upon this, and I feel bound to add that it seems to me exceeding the limits of legitimate enquiry to suggest anything of the kind.'

3. *Statement of Mrs. Edwards.*

'I am a sick nurse. I was in attendance on poor Mrs. Anderton all through her sickness. The poor lady was greatly cast down. She was expecting her death for weeks before it came. She seemed to think there was a doom on her. I do not think she had any suspicion that she was being poisoned. I am sure, poor dear lady, no one would ever think of poisoning her; everybody loved her too much. Mr. Anderton was dotingly fond of her. I never saw so good a husband in my life. I could have done anything for him, he was so good to his poor wife. I don't think he hardly ever left her. I used to be vexed sometimes, because, I said, he would not let me do anything for her. I mean he would not let me give her her slops or her physic. She took nothing but slops the best part of the time. She couldn't feel to relish anything at all, and meat made her sick. For the last two months or better I don't think she took anything from anybody, excepting it was from Mr. Anderton himself. He used to bring her her physic as regular as the clock struck, and everything from the kitchen was took first into his room, if he wasn't with the mistress, and he would carry it to her himself. He used to have rare work sometimes to get her to take anything. I am sure she wouldn't have done it, poor lady, for anyone but him. Not the last few weeks. She was so very sick and ill, and everything seemed to turn upon her stomach. Mr. Anderton always slept on a mattress in the mistress's room, so as to be within call. The mattress was put on the floor by the side of the bed, and nobody could have got to the bed without waking him. He was a very light sleeper. The least little sound used to wake him, and I often told him he was going the way to kill himself, and then what would our poor lady do? Once or twice I persuaded him to go out for a bit, and then he always insisted on my not leaving the room while he was away. Even when he was in his study he always made me stay with the lady; and if I wanted to go out for anything, I was to ring for him. Mrs. Anderton was never left without one or other of us for an hour, until the last six weeks; when she grew so bad, another nurse had to be got. Then we three did the same way between us. We were obliged to take her, because I was getting quite knocked up. How-

ever Mr. Anderton kept up the way he did,
I cannot think or say; but he broke down
altogether when the mistress died. I don't
think after that the poor gentleman was
ever quite right in his head. I remember
the doctor asking him one day whether
he had any tartar emetic in the house.
He said, No; but he would get some, if it
was wanted. Nothing more passed at the
time, so far as I know. It was brought
to my mind again by something which
happened after the poor lady's death. It
was nothing very particular; only I found
in her room a piece of paper, with " Tartar Emetic " printed on it. That was all
that was printed, but the word " Poison "
was written under it. I kept the paper
and showed it to the Baron. I don't know
why I did so; I suppose because he was
in the house at the time. Afterwards I
showed it to the lawyer, and he took
charge of it. I had no particular suspicion; none at all. I can't tell why I
took it up. I did it without thinking,
quite promiscuous like. I didn't show it

to master, because he was too ill to be worried.   That was the only reason.

'The above is the evidence I gave at the inquest.   I have nothing more to add.   I am quite sure that Mr. and Mrs. Anderton were very fond of each other.   I never saw two people so affectionate like.   The Baron was very fond of both of them.   I don't think Mrs. Anderton liked him much.   She seemed to have a sort of dread of him.   I don't know why; she never said so.   The Baron used often to call on Mr. Anderton, to see the doctor, but, so far as I know, he only saw the mistress once.   I think he knew she did not like him, and kept away on purpose.   He was a very kind-hearted gentleman.   He was always particularly polite and civil-spoken to me.   He used often to talk to me about master doting so on mistress.   He used to speak about his always giving her her physic and things. I remember one day his saying it wouldn't be very easy to give her anything unwholesome without his knowing of it, or something of that sort.   He seemed as if

he never could say enough in praise of
master, and I am sure he deserved it.   I
took him the paper I found just like I
might have taken it to master if he had
been well enough.   He was in the house
at the time.   He had been in the poor
lady's room with Dr. Dodsworth just before, and had stayed in the parlour to write
something.   He sent me into the room to
see if he had left his glove there.   It was
in looking for it that I saw the paper.   It
was lying just under the bed when I stooped
down to look for the glove.   I took it up
at first, thinking how careless it was to
have left it there when the room was put
straight after the poor lady died, and then
I saw what was written upon it.   The
glove was lying on the floor close to it.
There was no vallance to the bed; it had
been taken off for the sake of sweetness.   I
forget exactly what the Baron said when I
showed him the paper.   It was something
that made me think I might get into
trouble about it.   That was why I showed
it to the lawyer.   My brother had been to

him once before about some money that
ought to have come to us. He took the
paper to the magistrates, and that was how
the inquest came about.   I was very angry
about it, and so was the Baron. He asked
me how I could have been so foolish? I
don't know what made me think of taking
it to him.   I think it was something the
Baron said.   He did not advise me to do
it.   He did not advise me anything, but I
think he wanted me to burn it.   I offered
it to him, but he said he was afraid, or
something of that kind; and I think that
was what put it into my head to ask
the lawyer about it.'

4. *Memorandum by Mr. Henderson.*

The statement of the other nurse, herewith enclosed, merely corroborates that of
Mrs. Edwards, with respect to such matters
as came within her cognisance. I have,
therefore, not thought it necessary to insert
it here.

Mr. Prendergast's report, also enclosed,
is somewhat lengthy, and of a purely

technical character. It is to the following
effect :—

'1. That, on examination, the body of the
late Mrs. Anderton presented in all respects
the precise appearance which would be exhibited in a case of poisoning by antimony.

'2. It was, nevertheless, possible to account
for these appearances as the result of chronic 'gastritis,' or 'gastro-enteritis,' though
in some respects not such as either of those
diseases would be expected to present.

'3. The strictest and most thorough examination entirely failed in showing the
very slightest trace of either antimony or
arsenic; either in the contents of the various organs, or in the tissues.

'4. A portion of the medicine last taken
by the deceased was also examined, but
equally without result.

'5. From the lengthened period over
which the poisoning, if any, must have ex-
tended, and the small doses in which it
must have been administered, it is scarcely
possibly but that, had such really been the
case, some traces of it must have been

found in the tissues, though not perhaps in the contents of the stomach, &c.

'6. In a case of poisoning, also, the symptoms would have recurred in their severest form within a short period of taking the food or medicine in which it had been administered. In this case, however, they appear to have uniformly shown themselves at a late period of the night, and several hours after either food or medicine had been taken.

'7. It is therefore concluded that, notwithstanding the suspicious appearance of the body on dissection, death is to be attributed not to poison, but to an abnormal form of chronic 'gastro-enteritis,' for the peculiar symptoms of which the exceptional constitution of the deceased may in some degree account.'

5. *Statement of Police-Sergeant, Edward Reading.*

' I am a sergeant on the detective-staff of the Metropolitan Police. In October 1856, I was on duty at Notting Hill. I was em-

ployed to watch a gentleman by the name of
Anderton. He was in custody on a coroner's
warrant for the murder of his lady, but
couldn't be removed on account of being
ill. I was put in the house to prevent his
escape. I did not stay in his room. I did
at first, but it seemed of no use; so I spoke
to our superintendent, and got leave from
him to stop in the outer-room. I did this
to make things pleasant. I always try to
make things as pleasant as I can, compatible
with duty, especially when it's a gentleman.
It comes harder on them than on the regular hands, because they are not so much
used to it. In this case prisoner seemed to
take on terribly. He was very weak and
ill—too ill seemingly to get out of bed.
He used to lie with his eyes fixed upon one
corner of the room, muttering sometimes to
himself, but I couldn't tell what. He never
spoke to anyone. The only time he spoke
was once, to ask me to let him see the body.
I hadn't the heart to say no; but I went
with him and kept at the door. He could
hardly totter along, he was so weakly.

After about half-an-hour, I thought it was all very quiet, and looked in. He was lying on the floor in a dead faint, and I carried him back. He never spoke again, but lay just as I have said. Of course I took every precaution. Prisoner's room had two doors, one opening on the landing, and the other into the room where I stopped. I locked up the outer-door, and put three or four screws into it from the outside. The window was too high to break out at, but our men used to keep an eye upon it from the street. At night I used to lock the door of my room and stick open the door between the two. I was relieved occasionally by Sergeant Walsh,* but I mostly preferred seeing to it myself. I like to keep my own work in my own hands, and this was a very interesting case. When I first took charge I made a careful examination of the premises and of all papers, and the like. I found nothing to criminate

* The evidence of Sergeant Walsh is enclosed, but is merely corroborative of the present statement.— R. H.

the prisoner. I found a journal of the lady
who was murdered, with a note at the end
in his handwriting; but so far as it went
they seemed to be on very good terms. I
found also a lot of prescriptions and notes
referring to her illness, but no papers like
that found by the nurse, nor any traces of
powders or drugs of any kind. I went with
the nurse into the bed-room of the murdered
party, and made her point out the exact
spot where the paper was found. According to what she said it was lying just under
the bed on the right-hand side. The glove
was lying close to it, but not under the
bed. Somehow I didn't quite feel as if it
was all on the square. I thought the business of the paper looked rather queer. It
didn't seem quite feasible like. I have
known a thing of that sort by way of a
plant before now, so I thought I'd just go on
asking questions. That's always my way.
I ask all kinds of questions about everything, feeling my way like. I generally
find something turn up that way before I
have done. Something turned up this

time. I don't know that it was much—
perhaps not. I have my own opinion about
that. This is how it was. After more
questions of one kind and another, I got to
something that led me to ask the nurse
which side of the bed Mr. Anderton usually
went to give the lady food and physic.
She and the other servants all agreed that,
being naturally left-handed like, he always
went to the *left*-hand side of the bed, so as
he could get to feed her with a spoon. He
was very bad with his right hand. Couldn't
handle a spoon with it no more than some
of us could with the left. Nurse said she
had seen him try once or twice, which he
always spilled everything. I mean of course
with his right hand. He was handy enough
with his left. When I heard this, I began
to suspect we might be on a false scent.
This is the way I looked at it. The glove,
as I told you, was lying on the floor by the
right side of the bed, so as anybody who
dropped it must have been standing on
that side which it's the natural side to go
to as being nearest the door. The paper

was close to it, just under the same side of
the bed. Now, I took it as pretty clear
prisoner hadn't put that paper there for
the purpose, but if he'd done it at all, he
had dropped it by accident in giving the
stuff. I fancy, too, he'd naturally be particularly careful in giving that sort of stuff
not to spill it about the place, so he'd be
pretty well sure to take his best hand to it.
In that case he'd have dropped it on the
left-hand side of the bed—not the right.
Still, of course it might have got blown
across, or, for the matter of that, kicked,
though that was not very likely, as the bed
was a wide one, and put in a sort of recess
like, quite out of any sort of draught. So
I thought I'd have another look at the
place, and, poking about under the bed, I
found a long narrow box, which the servants
told me was full of bows and arrows, and
hadn't been moved out of its place since
they first came to the house. It took up
the whole length of the bed within a foot
or so, and lay right along the middle, on
the floor. There was a mark along the

floor that showed how long it had been
there. A bit of paper like that never could
have got blown right over that without
touching it, if there had been ever such a
draught. When I'd got so far, I fancied
things began to look very queer; so I got
the bed shifted out of its place altogether.
The coffin was in the way, and I got that
moved to one side of the room, and pulled
the bed right clear of the box. As we
shifted the coffin, I thought I saw something
like a piece of paper under the flannel
shroud. I said nothing at the time, but
waited until the undertaker's men were out
of the room and I was alone. I then
opened the shroud and found a small folded
paper: it was put just under the hands,
which were crossed over the bosom of the
corpse. I opened it and found a lock of
hair, which I saw directly was Mr. Anderton's, and there were a few words in writing, which I copied down, in my note-book;
and then I put the hair and the paper and
all back where I found them. The writing
was, " Pray for me, darling, pray for me."

I knew the hand at once for Mr. Anderton's. His writing is very remarkable, by reason, I suppose, of being so left-handed. Of course that wasn't evidence, but somehow I got an idea out of it that a man wouldn't go on in that way with his wife just after he'd been and murdered her. It struck me that that would be against nature, leastways if he was in his right mind. After I had finished with the coffin, I took a look at the box. As I expected, the top was covered ever so thick with dust, and it was pretty clear that, at all events, the bit of paper had never lain a-top of it. I put a piece just like it on to try, and blew it off again; and it made a great mark and got all dirty. The paper picked up by the nurse was quite clean, or very nearly so. Putting all this together I came pretty nigh a conclusion that, at all events, it wasn't Mr. Anderton as had dropped the paper there. The sides of the box were also dusty, but there were marks on them like as if a brush or a broom had brushed against them. I put the box and the bed back into their places, and went

down to question the housemaid.* I found
that she had put the room tidy the day
Mrs. Anderton died, and had passed a short
hair-broom under the bed, as there were
several things lying about. She said she
was quite sure there was no bit of paper
there then, as she had stooped down and
looked under. I tried with the same broom,
and you couldn't reach the box without
stooping, as she said. I then enquired who
had been in the room between the time of
the death and the finding of the paper.
No one had been there but the nurse, the
doctor, the housemaid, and Baron R**. I
was determined to hunt it out if possible.
I questioned the nurse and the housemaid
—on the quiet, not to excite suspicion—
but felt pretty clear they knew nothing
more about it; and when next Baron R**
came I sounded him about different points.
He did not seem to know that Mr. Anderton was so left-handed, nor could I get any
information from him on the subject. He

* The housemaid's deposition corroborates this
part of the evidence.

didn't seem at first to see what I was driving at, and, of course, I didn't mean he should; but after a while I saw he had struck out the same idea as I had about the place where the paper was found, though I had not meant to let him into that. He seemed quite struck of a heap by it. I fancied at the moment that he turned regularly pale, but he was just blowing his nose with a large yellow silk handkerchief, and I could not be sure. He said nothing to me of what he had guessed, nor did I to him. I like to keep those things as quiet as I can, particularly from parties' friends. I have not been able to get any further clue, but I am convinced that something is to be made out of that paper business yet. I generally know a scent when I get on one, and my notion is that I am on one now. I did not see the Baron again until the evening before Mr. Anderton made away with himself. He came then in a great hurry, and insisted on seeing the prisoner. I said I would ask, but did not expect he could, as Mr. Anderton would see or speak to no one.

He seemed to be in a sad state, partly with exhaustion after waiting on his wife so long, and partly with the worry of having this hanging over him.   He was a very sensitive gentleman, and seemed to take it more to heart than anyone I ever saw.   He wouldn't see any one, not even his lawyer.   When I told him about the Baron, however, he said he might come in, and they were together half-an-hour or more.   I did not hear anything that passed.   When the Baron came out, he took me on one side and told me everything was all right, and his friend was sure to get off.   He said he was quite overpowered with the good news, and particularly begged that he might not be disturbed by anyone, as he thought he could sleep now.   He had hardly slept a wink all the time.   I promised not to disturb him, and he lay quite quiet all night.   I peeped in once or twice to make sure he was there, but did not speak.   I noticed a faint smell like peaches once, but did not think anything of it.   In the morning I went in to take him his breakfast, and found him dead and quite cold. In his hand was a little bottle which had contained prussic acid, and which had evidently come out of a pocket medicine-chest that lay on the bed. I gave the alarm, and the divisional surgeon was sent for; but he was stone dead. At about nine o'clock the Baron's servant came round to know whether he had left a pocket medicine-chest the night before. I questioned the servant, and found the Baron had given him a list of the places where he had been, and that he had asked at several already. The medicine-chest wanted proved to be the one found in Mr. Anderton's room. 'On the pillow I found also a piece of paper in Mr. Anderton's handwriting, of which I enclose a copy.'

6. *Pencil note found on the pillow of Mr. Anderton.*

' Let no man condemn me for what I do. God knows how I have fought against it. My darling! my own darling! have I not seen you night and day by my side beckon-ing me to come? Not while a chance

remained. Not while there was one hope
left to escape this doom of hideous disgrace,
which dogs me to the death. No, darling,
my honour—*your husband's* honour before
all. It is over now. No chance—no hope
—only ignominy, shame, death. I come,
darling. *You* know whether I am guilty
of this horrible charge. My darling—my
own darling—I see you smile at the very
thought. God bless you for that smile.
God pardon me for what I am about to do.
God reunite us, darling.'

Section VII.

1.—*Statement of Mr. Henderson.*

In the concluding portion of the evidence we have now a double object in view. First, to lay before you the various links by which the circumstances, already detailed, are connected into a single chain; and secondly, to elucidate the general bearing of the whole upon the particular case of the death of Madame R**, into which it is my more immediate duty to enquire. It was this apparent connection with the entire story which first led me to investigate matters otherwise quite beyond my province, and you will, I have no doubt, after reading the evidence, concur in the propriety of my so doing.

It is unfortunate that, in this important part of the case, as previously with regard to the no less important point of the suspicious circumstances attendant on Madame

R**'s first illness at Bognor, the evidence
of the principal witnesses is open to very
grave question. It is not indeed, as then,
that the moral character of the individuals
themselves rests under any suspicion, for,
so far as I have been able to learn, both the
servant-of-all-work, and her lover, John
Styles, are perfectly respectable people;
whilst the young man, Aldridge, though certainly a foolish and perhaps rather a dissi-
pated young fellow, has a very fair character from the house of business in which he
is now employed. But the evidence of the
two former is, as will be seen, greatly di-
minished in value by the circumstances
under which it was obtained, whilst, in the
latter, there is so clear a suspicion of *animus*
as cannot but throw still greater doubts upon evidence in itself sufficiently questionable—and rendered yet more so by other
circumstances which will hereafter more
fully appear.

It was this man Aldridge, whose letter,
as you will remember, led to the investigation, of which the result is now before you;

and his statement, hereto annexed, that first gave substance to the suspicions of foul play on the part of the Baron, and, in conjunction with the discovery of the enclosed papers, subsequently induced me to extend my enquiries to the cases of Mr. and Mrs. Anderton. I confess that, notwithstanding the doubt with which his statement is surrounded, I am still inclined to accept it as substantially true, though possibly somewhat coloured by personal feeling against the Baron. The point, however, has seemed to me of sufficient importance to justify the occupying a considerable portion of this present division of the case, with such evidence as I have been able to gather respecting the circumstances of his final ejectment; and it will be for you to determine between the story as told by himself and that of Baron R**.

With regard to the other two witnesses, who, by one of those singular coincidences that, in criminal cases, seem so often to occur, are able to confirm in some degree the evidence of Aldridge, there is, I think, less

difficulty.   They had certainly no business
where they were, but the circumstances are
such as to fully acquit them of any felo-
nious intent, while, even had such existed, it
would be difficult to see how the fact of
such intent could have exercised any influence over their present statements.   It is,
moreover, quite clear that there has been no
collusion upon the subject.

I have now only to refer, in conclusion,
to the fragment of paper found in the Baron's
rooms in Russell Place, and the marked copy
of the ' Zoïst,' belonging to the late Mr.
Anderton, to which Mr. Morton referred in
his statement * as having formed the subject
of discussion at Mr. Anderton's house on the
evening of October 13, 1854.   The first
of these is a portion of a letter, which
I have endeavoured, so far as possible,
to complete.   Admitting that I have done
so correctly, and coupling it with the fact
of the visit which, as I have been able to
ascertain, was paid by a foreign lady to
the Baron ' very early in the morning' fol-

* Section II., 2.

P

lowing the death of Madame R**, it appears to throw no inconsiderable light upon the extraordinary circumstances of the death of Madame R**. The bearing of the second document on the case will be perhaps less clear. I have no hesitation in admitting that when the connection first suggested itself to my own mind, I at once dismissed it as too absurd to be entertained for a moment. But I feel bound to add, that the further my enquiries have progressed, the more strongly this apparent connection has forced itself upon me as the only clue to a maze of coincidences such as it has never before been my lot to encounter; and that while even now unable to accept it as a fact, I find it still more impossible to thrust it altogether on one side. I have, therefore, left the matter for your decision, merely pointing out, as I have before, in the opening portion of my report, that, even admitting the influence of these passages upon the mind of the Baron, and the ultimate success of the plan founded upon their suggestion, that success, however extraordinary, may not necessarily involve, as at first appears, the admission of those monstrous assertions of the 'mesmeric' journal on which it was based.

With these observations, I now submit to your consideration the concluding portion of the evidence; after which, it will only be necessary for me to take a brief review of the whole case before leaving it finally in your hands.

2.—*Statement of Mrs. Jackson.*

'My name is Mary Jackson. I live in Goswell Street, City Road. I am a monthly and sick-nurse. In June 1856, I was engaged to nurse Madame R**. I was recommended to the Baron by Dr. Marsden, who lodged in the same house. I have often nursed for him. Madame R** was not very ill. I don't think she was ill enough to require a nurse. Of course she was the better for one—everybody always is—but she could have done without one. I came by the Baron's wish. He was anxious like. The poor gentleman was very fond of his wife. I never saw such a good husband.

I am sure no other husband would have
done what he did, and she so cold to him.
I don't think she cared about him at all.
She hardly ever spoke to him unless it was
when he spoke first. She never spoke much.
She always seemed frightened; especially
when the Baron was there. She certainly
seemed to be afraid of him, but I can't tell
why. He was always kind to her. He was
the nicest and most civil-spoken gentleman
I ever knew. It was not that he was not
particular. Quite the reverse. I wish all
husbands were half so particular, and then
nurses wouldn't so often get into trouble.
Everything used to be done like clockwork.
Every morning he used to give me a paper
what was to be given in the day. I mean
medicine and food. A list of everything,
with the time it was to be taken. Everything used to be ready, and I used to give
it regular. No one else ever used to give
anything. *The Baron never gave anything
himself.* Never at all. I am quite sure of
that. He used to say that it was nurse's
business, and so it is. He often said he had

seen so much sickness he had learned never to interfere with the nurse, and I only wish all other gentlemen would do the same. He used to be very particular about the physic. We always have the bottles for our perquisite. We get a shilling a dozen for them all round, if they are clean. The Baron objected to this. He allowed me a shilling a dozen instead. The bottles were all put away in a cupboard. They never used to be quite emptied. The Baron always made a point of having fresh in before the old was quite finished. He said he always liked to have them to refer to in case of accident or mistake. He was a very careful gentleman. I nursed Madame R** every day until her recovery. I am quite certain that, during the hours I was there, nothing was ever given to her but what passed through my hands.'

3.—*Statement of Mrs. Ellis.*

'My name is Jane Ellis. I am a sick-nurse, and live in Goodge Street, Tottenham Court Road. At about the end of July

1856, I was engaged as night nurse to Madame R**. Perhaps she did not exactly require one. She was ill, but she could help herself. At times she was very ill. It was much more comfortable for her, and she could afford it. Baron R** never seemed to spare anything for her. She was generally worst at night. The worst attacks used to come on about every fortnight. It was generally on a Saturday. I took turn and turn about with Mrs. Jackson. She took the day-work, and I took the night. I used to come at ten o'clock, and leave at breakfast-time. During that time I was never out of the room. It was the Baron's particular desire. When I first came he made it a condition that I should never leave the room, and never go to sleep. He was the most particular gentleman I ever nursed for. I have nothing whatever to say against him. Quite the contrary. He was always civil and pleasant-spoken, and behaved most handsome, as a gentleman should do. He was uncommon fond of the lady. She didn't seem to care much about him. She was ill, poor soul, and could not care about anybody. She seemed quite frightened like. When the Baron came into the room she used to follow him about with her eyes, as if she was afraid of him. I never heard him say an unkind word. Other times she would lie quite quiet, and not speak a word for hours. She seemed afraid of everybody. If I moved about the room, I could see her eyes following me about and watching me everywhere. I think it was part of her complaint. The Baron was most attentive. I never saw such an attentive husband. He used to lie in the next room. It opened into the bedroom, and he always had the door wide open. He was a wonderfully light sleeper. If either of us spoke a word, he would be in the room directly to ask what was the matter. I couldn't even move across the room, but what he would hear it. He was a wonderful man. He seemed to live almost without sleep. I think it must have been the meat did it. He used to eat enormous quantities of meat. I never saw a man eat so much. When I first came he used to joke with me about it. Madame R** was not so bad then, and we used to talk sometimes. He told me it was because he was a mesmeriser. I don't believe in mesmerism. I told him so. He didn't say anything; he only laughed. One night he offered to send me to sleep. That was when I had been there about a week. I said he might try if he could. He looked hard at me, ever so long, and made some odd motions with his hands. I did go to sleep. I don't believe it was mesmerism. Of course not. I think it was looking at his eyes. I told him so. He asked if he should do it again. He did it once more. That was the night after. I went to sleep then almost directly. Of course, I knew it was not mesmerism, but I couldn't help it. He did not talk about it any more. He only said I must take care not to go to sleep of my own accord. I did drop asleep three or four times after that. That was not from anything the Baron did. He was not in the room at the

time. He must have been in the next room.
I suppose the door was open. It always
was. The first time I went to sleep was
about a week after we had talked about the
mesmerism. It was on a Saturday night
or Friday. I am not quite sure which. It
was one of the nights when Madame R**
was so ill. She had gone to sleep at about
eleven o'clock. She seemed very well then.
She was sleeping quite quiet. I suppose I
must have dropped off. I was awoke by
her moaning in her sleep. That was about
one o'clock. She soon woke up in great
pain, and had a very bad attack. The
Baron came into the room just as I awoke.
Something woke him, and he came in directly. He told me what it was that woke
him. It was me snoring. He said so. I
fell asleep again a fortnight after in the same
way. The Baron was not there. Madame
R** was asleep. She had not slept for
many nights. I must have dropped off in
a doze hearing her so nicely asleep. The
Baron woke me. That was at about one
o'clock. He was very much displeased. He

told me Madame R** had been walking in her sleep and might have killed herself. He said she went into the kitchen. I am certain that was where he said. I can swear it. He asked what I had taken for supper, and tasted what was left of the beer. He seemed very much vexed and disturbed. I was very sorry, and promised to be very careful another time. I never had such a thing happen in any other case, and I told him so. He said he would look over it that time, but it must never happen again. He went up-stairs afterwards. I think it was to speak to somebody. He said somebody had seen her, I think. Madame R** was ill that night. She began to moan while we were talking, and had a very bad attack. The Baron said she must have caught cold, and I am afraid she did. I determined to be particularly careful for the time to come. I was very careful for some time, particularly when she was asleep. She hardly slept at all for two weeks, but when she did I was very careful. At the end of that time I must have fallen asleep again. I was hardly aware of it. I know I must have been asleep, because when I looked at the clock it was two hours later than I thought. Madame R** was ill again that night. I was very much vexed. I began to think somebody was playing tricks upon me. It was so strange, coming every fortnight. I did not tell the Baron. I know it was wrong, but I was afraid. Next fortnight I was on the look-out. Madame R** went to sleep again. I was determined not to go to sleep. I thought somebody must have played tricks with the beer, so I wouldn't drink it. I ate no supper, and drank nothing but some strong green tea I made for myself. I was quite sure the tea must keep me awake. It did not. I awoke with a great start about one o'clock, and found Madame R** bad again as usual. I was very much bothered about it. I made up my mind to tell the Baron if it happened again. It did happen again, but I did not tell him. Madame R** was so bad then I was really afraid; and, after that, it never happened again, and she got well. I know I ought to have told the Baron. I am very sorry I did not. Such a thing never happened to me before. Of course I have slept in a sick-room before, but not when it was against orders. I was there about three months. I dropped asleep in that way, I think, six times; but I am not quite sure. It was always while Madame R** was asleep. She was always bad afterwards. I did not say anything to her about it, or about her walking. The Baron particularly desired I would not. He said it would frighten her. He never asked me again whether I had been asleep, or I would have told him. I was really going to tell him once or twice, but something always happened to stop me. I can swear that nothing of the kind ever happened to me before. There must have been something wrong. I have sick-nursed twenty years, and have the best characters from many doctors and patients.' *

* This I find to be the case.—R. H.

4.—*Statement of Mr. Westmacott.*

'London, September 20, 1857.

'SIR,

'I have the honour to inform you that in compliance with your request, I have submitted to the most careful and searching examination and analysis the contents of three dozen and seven (43) medicine phials forwarded by you for that purpose.

'The number and contents of these phials correspond exactly with the prescriptions, &c., furnished by Messrs. Andrews and Empson,* and after the most exact analysis I have been unable to detect the slightest trace of either arsenic, antimony, or any similar substance.

'I have the honour to be,

'Your most obedient servant,

'THOMAS WESTMACOTT,
'Analytical Chemist.'

---

* The chemists from whom the Baron obtained his medicines.—R. H.

5.—*Statement of Henry Aldridge.*

'My name is Henry Aldridge. I am a clerk, in the employ of Messrs. Simpson and Co., City. In the summer of 1856 I came to lodge at Mrs. Brown's in Russell Place. I did not come there first as a lodger, but as a friend of her son. I had known him in Australia. We were together in the same store in Melbourne, and got to be great friends. We did not come home in the same ship. That is a mistake. I came home some weeks before he did, and was in Liverpool when he arrived. I think he came in the Lightning, but cannot be sure. I used to board so many ships, that I can't call to mind. I was in a Liverpool house then for a time, and it was my duty to board every ship as she came up. I agreed to go with him to London. I could not go directly, as I had to give notice to my employers, but I was to follow him. He asked me to stay with him for his wedding at his mother's house, and I did so. That was how I first came

to Russell Place. After that he arranged
with his mother for me to take a room
regularly; and I was to pay so much a
week, and so much more when I got a
situation. I was not aware of the Baron
making any objection. I saw very little
of him. I slept on the floor above, and
was always very careful not to make any
noise on account of Madame R**. She
was ill, and I took particular care not to
disturb her. I used sometimes to be out
late. I have been intoxicated in my life.
Not very often. Not often at all. Never
while I was in Russell Place. I have been
out to my friends while I was there, and have
drunk wine and spirits, but never to be the
worse for it. I may have been merry.
I don't say I have not been once or twice
a little excited with wine. What I mean
is, that I have never been in such a state
as not to be quite conscious of what I
was doing, and quite able to control myself. I am quite certain that I never
made the slightest disturbance, or could
have done so without knowing it. That

I will swear to. I believe the Baron accused me of it to Mrs. Brown. He spoke to her several times about it, and wished her to turn me out. She said she had never seen anything wrong, and couldn't say anything till she did, because I was her son's friend. At last he got her to do it. The reason was that I was found by a policeman on the doorstep at about twelve o'clock one night insensible. The policeman knocked and rang, and woke up the house, and the Baron said I was drunk. I was perfectly sober. I had had nothing whatever but one small bottle of ale. The facts of the case were these, and I will swear to them. I had been kept late at our office with some heavy correspondence, and had then walked home with another clerk from the same office— William Wells—having taken nothing but one small bottle of ale, which I had at a public-house in High Holborn, as I felt quite tired. Wells had some brandy-and-water. He left me at the corner of Tottenham Court Road. When I got to Russell

Place I tried to open the door with my
latch-key, but the latch was fastened. I
then rang at the bell, but could not make it
sound, and the handle came out loose, as if
the wire was broken. I tried the key once
more, and was just thinking whether I
should not go to some place, as I did not
like to disturb Madame R** by knocking,
when the door was opened from the inside.
I turned round to go in, when something
was thrust into my face, and I can remember nothing more. I must have fallen down
insensible, and the policeman found me.
This is the truth. I could not see who
opened the door. There was a street-lamp
close to the area-gate, but the person was
in the shadow. I cannot account for it. I
made sure at the time it was a trick of the
Baron to get me turned out. I think so
still, but am not so sure of it as I was.
What I mean is, that, on reflection, I don't
think it is certain enough to accuse him of
such a thing. I will swear to the truth of
what I have said. I will swear that I was
perfectly sober—as sober as I am now. My

employers and Will Wells can prove it. I
do not know why the Baron should have
wished so much to turn me out. We never
had words about anything. I don't think I
ever spoke to him but once. I mean, not
more than "Good morning," or such like.
That was on the occasion about which I
wrote to the Assurance Office after Madame
R**'s death. It was one Saturday night.
I had had a half-holiday, and had been up
to Putney in a boat with some friends. We
had drunk a good deal of beer and shandy-
gaff, but I was not drunk. I was quite
sober, though perhaps a little excited. Nothing to speak of. I got home at about eleven
o'clock. I had a latch-key then, but the
lock was hampered; and when I got back
home I found the servant-girl sitting up to
let me in. I went up very quietly, not to
disturb Madame R**. I saw her bedroom-
door ajar as I passed. The door of the
room next to it was wide open, and there was
some sort of lamp burning. No one moved
or said anything as I went by. I took off
my shoes to go more softly; but the house

was old, and it was impossible to move without the stairs creaking a little. The stairs below the Baron's room were stone, and did not creak. I had a candle, which I shaded carefully with my hand. I went to bed; but I suppose I was over-tired, for I could not get to sleep. The night was very hot. When I had been in bed about a couple of hours I thought I would have a good wash, and see if that would cool me. I got up and went to the washhand-stand. I found the jug empty. The maid often forgot to fill it. I took the jug, and went out on to the landing to fill it at the tap. I went very softly, not to disturb Madame R**. As I got on to the landing, I saw some one coming out of her room, and went to look over the bannister. From the landing of my room you can see that of the floor below. I looked over, and saw that it was Madame R**. She was in her dressing-gown, but had no candle. She went to the stairs, and there I lost sight of her. As I watched her past the door of the other room, I saw the shadow of a man's head and shoulders upon the wall, as if somebody was watching her. I leaned against the bannister to watch her, and it creaked, and the shadow vanished directly. When I looked up again it was gone, and at first I thought it must have been fancy; but I am quite certain about it now. I was only doubtful for the moment. It was so sudden. I could swear to it now. I saw it perfectly plain. I saw it all the time Madame R** was going down the first flight of stairs. About twelve of them. She was at the corner when I turned and leaned over to watch her. I felt convinced that Madame R** was walking in her sleep. The staircase was quite dark beyond the corner, and she had walked straight down. I was afraid she would hurt herself, and went down to the Baron's door. He was asleep; at least, I had to knock twice. He then came to the door, and I told him what I had seen. He seemed a good deal annoyed, and at once took up the lamp and went down stairs. I looked over the bannister, and saw him go down. From that place you can see right down to the door which leads to the kitchen-stairs. There is a glass partition between them and the hall. I saw him go in at the door, and I saw the light through the glass as he went part of the way down stairs. Presently he came up again, and stood back from the door while Madame R** came up past him, and walked up stairs; and he then followed her. When I saw her coming up, I went back to my own landing and looked over. She went back to her own room, fast asleep still, as it seemed to me, and he followed. I heard whispering in the room, and then the Baron came up to me. He thanked me very much for telling him, and said that Madame R** had gone down into the kitchen, and was just coming out as he got to the foot of the stairs. He particularly begged me never to mention it, as it might come to her ears and do her harm; and I have never spoken of it to any one till I wrote to the Assurance Office. I had almost forgotten all about it, when it was recalled to my mind by seeing that poor Madame R** had killed herself in a sleep-

walking fit. I then wrote. I had no malice against the Baron, nor have I now. I
don't know why he tried to turn me out. I
suppose he really thought I disturbed his
wife. He was very fond of her, and I dare
say he was anxious and fretful about her. I
was very angry at the time, but when I
come to think of it, I dare say I was hard
upon him. He never seemed to bear me
any grudge about what I have seen. On
the contrary, he always said he was very
much obliged to me. This is all I know on
the subject, and I can swear to the truth of
every word. I am quite positive he said
Madame R** had been into the kitchen.'

6.—*Statement of Miles Thompson.*

'I am a police-constable. In August
1856, I used to be on night duty in Russell
Place. I remember Baron R** speaking to
me one night, and asking me to keep a look
out as often as I could of a night to keep
the street quiet. He gave me five shillings
for my extra trouble. I was on the beat
one night, about twelve o'clock, when I saw

some one lying on the Baron's door-step. It was a young gentleman, and at first I thought he was dead; but found he was only insensible. I set him up against the railings, and was going to ring the bell, when I saw a latch-key in his hand. I tried it in the door, and it opened it directly, and I took him into the hall. I then knocked and rang till somebody came. The bell rang quite well. The Baron came down in his dressing-gown, and two or three other people. I offered to go for a doctor, but the Baron said he was only drunk. I helped to carry him up-stairs, and get him into bed. The Baron gave me half-a-crown for my trouble. He seemed very much annoyed, as was natural, and said he wished I had taken the young man to the station. I think he was drunk myself. He smelt a little of beer, but not much. I helped to put him to bed, and went away. That is all I know.'

[N.B.—By letters from Messrs. Simpson and Mr. Wells, Mr. Aldridge's assertion that he was sober is borne out up to the time of the latter's leaving him at the corner of Tottenham Court Road, certainly not more than half-an-hour before he was found as above stated by Police-constable Thompson.—R. H.]

7.—*Statement of John Johnson.*

' to

' mister endusson sir obeadent to yore Comands i hev eksammd tha belwir in russle please wich in my humbel Hopinnium it hev ben Templd wit by sum Hunperfeshnl And wich tha Wir it hev ben tuk hof tha .Kranke & putt bak hall nohowlik wich hany Purfeshnl And wud be a Shammd fur 2 du It i am sur yore hobeadnt survnt too Comand

'jon jonsun
' Plommr hand belanger
' totunmcort rode
' lundon '

8.—*Statement of Susan Turner.*

' My name is Susan Turner. In August 1856, I was general servant to Mrs. Brown in Russell Place. I remember the night that Madame R** came down-stairs. I

had sat up to let Mr. Aldridge in because
the latch was broken. Mistress broke it
that afternoon. I don't suppose the Baron
knew anything about it. Mr. Aldridge
came in rather late. I cannot justly say
the time. He was quite right. I mean
quite sober. He went straight up to bed. I
did not go up to bed. My young man was
in the kitchen. He is a very respectable
young man, upon a railway. I don't know
what railway. I know he goes to Scotland
sometimes with his engine, that is all. He
is what they call a fireman. He was
going down with a luggage-train somewhere that night very late, and came to see
me. Mistress didn't know he was there.
He came in after she was gone to bed. He
was to start at two, and we sat till about
one. He was just going away, and we
were standing at the kitchen-door, when we
heard somebody in the hall. I said, " Oh,
Lor! that 's missis." He said, " She'll be
coming to look for you," and wanted me to
go and meet her while he cut out by the
area. I said, No, that wouldn't do, by

reason of its being all glass, and a gas-lamp at top of the area-steps.* I pulled him along to the lumber-room. The lumber-room is behind the kitchen and the cellar. There are some old boxes and things there, but nobody ever goes into it. I thought my mistress would not think of looking there. Just as we got to the door, we saw somebody come from the hall and down the stairs. I whispered to John, "Why, that's not missis—that's Madame." My mistress was very tall and stout, and Madame R** was small and thin. I could see her as she came through the door, because there was some sort of light in the hall. She came right down-stairs and passed where we were. She went right on into the little place at the end where the Baron kept all his bottles and stuff. She did not go into the kitchen. Not at all. I will swear to that. She went into the Baron's place.

---

* The arrangement alluded to will be seen from the frontispiece. The inner partition is entirely of glass, while the outer has a row of large panes along the top.—R. H.

'I could see her as she came through the door, because
there was some sort of light in the hall. She came
right down-stairs and passed where we were.'

The laboratory, I dare say it is; I don't know. It was where the bottles are. John and me crept to the window and looked out. The window of the lumber-room looks right into the window of the back-room where the bottles are. You could see in quite plain. It was a bright moonlight night, and there is a sort of tin looking-glass over the back-room window to make more light like. We saw Madame go into the room and take a bottle from a shelf. She poured out a glassful and drank it. Then she put the bottle back in its place. It was the last on the second shelf. Then she went out again; and when we turned round we saw a light shining into the room from the kitchen-stairs. It stayed there till Madame had gone past our door again, and then it went up again. Just as it got to the top of the stairs I peeped out, and saw it was the Baron. Madame was close behind him. I said to John, " Why, John, there's the Baron." He said he supposed he had come to look after his wife. After they had gone, John and me went into the bottle-place.

We found the glass on the table. There
were a few drops of stuff in it. John and
me smelt it, and it was just like wine. It
tasted just like wine, too. Then we looked
for the bottle. It was at the end of the
second shelf. It was about half-full of stuff
that looked like wine. There was something in gold letters on the bottle. I can't
tell what it was. It was " vin " something.
I know that, because John and me settled
it must mean wine. I think I should know
the rest if I saw it '—[being here shown
several labels, witness here picked out the
following: 'Vin. Ant. Pot. Tart.'—design-
ating antimonial wine, a mixture of sherry
and tartar-emetic]—'I am pretty sure that
was the one. I remember it because they
were such funny words. I remember John
and me joking about " pots and pies."
The stuff in the bottle smelt just like wine.
It was just like sherry wine. I did not
taste that. John wouldn't let me. He
said I might go and poison myself for
aught I knew. We put the bottle back,
and then John went away. I said nothing

about it to anybody.   Not even when Madame was taken ill that night.   I was afraid, by reason of John.   I have never said a word about it to any living soul till I was asked to-day.   Certainly not to Mr. Aldridge, nor he to me.   I will swear to the truth of all I have said.   I am quite positive that Madame never went near the kitchen. I am quite positive that the Baron must have seen her come out of the bottle-place.   He was standing with the candle in his hand waiting for her.   That I can swear.'

[N.B.—The statement of the 'young man' referred to fully corroborates the above statement.   The accompanying plan (see frontispiece) will make this witness's evidence more clear.—R. H.]

9.—*Copy of a Letter from a leading Mesmerist to the compiler, with reference to the power claimed by mesmeric operators over those subjected to their influence.*

'Dorset Square.

'MY DEAR SIR,—

. . . . . . Many times after throwing Sarah Parsons into the mesmeric state, I have *willed* her to go into a dark room and pick up a pin or other article equally minute, and however powerless she might be at the time out of the state was quite immaterial. My will and power being employed was sufficient. Then, Mr. L——, a paralytic, under my influence, without losing conciousness or undergoing any recognisable change, has many times, with the lame leg, stepped up on to and down again from an ordinary dining-room chair. This, of course, was a master-piece of mesmeric manipulation. I wish I could write more and better, but my eyes forbid * * *

'With kindest regards,

'Yours most truly,

'D. HANDS.'

10.—*Fragment of a Letter found in the Baron's room after the death of Madame R*∴.*

[FACSIMILE.]

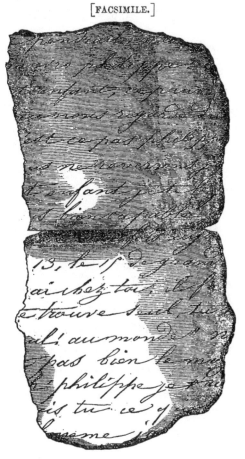

[THE WRITING ON THE FRAGMENT.]

.....pendrait n'e...........................
....auvre philippe? E...................
.....t enfant, ce pauvre...................
....ui nous regarde du...................
.....est ce pas philipp.................
......us ne reverrons ja.................
.....t enfant je te le j...................
......is bien capable j.................
......core une fois, aujo...................
.....13, le 15, de grand.................
....rai chez toi; il fa...................
...e trouve seul, tu ı...................
.....ul au monde! n'...................
......pas bien le moy.................
.....h! philippe je t'ai....................
.....is tu ce qu...................
....emme ja...................

[THE WRITING COMPLETED.]

.........On (?)

te...pendrait n'e...st ce pas mon
p...auvre philippe? E...h bien par
ce...t enfant, ce pauvre...petit ange (?)
q...ui nous regarde du...haut du ciel,
n'...est ce pas philipp...e et que
no...us ne reverrons ja...mais, par
ce...t enfant je te le j...ure. Tu m'en
sa...is bien capable j...e crois.
En...core une fois, aujo...urd'hui c'est
le...13, le 15, de grand...matin je
se...rai chez toi; il fa...ut que je
t...e trouve seul, tu ı...ne comprends;
se...ul au monde! n'...en sais
tu ... pas bien le moy ... en ?
O...h! philippe je t'ai...me (je t'aime?)
sa...is tu ce qu...e c'est qu' une
f...emme ja...louse ?—

Translation.

'(They) would hang thee, would they not, my poor Philip? Well, by that child—that poor (little angel) who is now—is it not so, Philip?—looking down on us from heaven, and whom we shall never see again: by that child I swear it to you. Once more. To-day is the 13th. On the 15th, very early in the morning, I shall be at your house. I must find you alone—you understand me, alone in the world! Do you not well know the means? Oh, Philip, I love thee (I love thee?). Knowest thou what a jealous woman is?

11.—*Extracts from the '*Zoïst Magazine,*'* *No. XLVII., for October* 1854.

'MESMERIC CURE OF A LADY WHO HAD BEEN TWELVE YEARS IN THE HORIZONTAL POSITION, WITH EXTREME SUFFERING. By the Rev. R. A. F. Barrett, B.D., Senior Fellow of the King's College, Cambridge.

* * * * *

'In January 1852, I was calling upon

——, when she happened to tell me that she had been in considerable pain for a fortnight past; that the only thing that relieved her was mesmerism; but the friend who used to mesmerise her was gone.   .   .

.   .   .   I continued to mesmerise her occasionally for some months.   .   .   .

'*April* 21*st*.—I kept her asleep an hour and a quarter in the morning and the same in the evening. She said* her throat looked parched and feverish; at her request, *I ate some black currant paste, which she said moistened it.*   .   .   .   She said, "Before you ate, my stomach was contracted and had a queer-looking sort of moisture in it; now the stomach is its full size and does not look shrunk, and part of the moisture is gone."

'I. "But you could not *get nourishment* so?"

'A. "Yes: *I could get all my system wants.*"

*   *   *   *   *

* In a former portion of the case we are told that this patient was *clairvoyant,* and could see her own internal condition.—R. H.

'*April* 26*th*.—In the evening I kept her asleep one hour, *and took tea for her.*

'*April* 27*th*. . . . *I ate dinner*, and *she felt* much stronger.

  * * * * *

'I kept her asleep two hours and a quarter in the morning and one hour in the evening, *eating for her as usual.*'

SECTION VIII.

CONCLUSION.

THERE now only remains for me, in conclusion, to sum up as briefly and succinctly as possible the evidence contained in the preceding statements. In so doing, it will be necessary to adopt an arrangement somewhat different from that which has been hitherto followed. Each step of the narrative will therefore be accompanied with a marginal reference to the particular deposition from which it may be taken.

First, then, for what may be called the preliminary portions of the evidence. With these we need here deal but very briefly.   They consist almost en-   I. tirely of letters, furnished by the courtesy of a near relation of the late Mrs. Anderton, and read as follows: Some six or seven-and-twenty years ago, the mother of Mrs. Anderton — Lady Boleton — after giving birth to twin daughters, under circumstances of a peculiarly exciting and agitating nature, died in child-bed. Both Sir Edward Boleton and herself appear to have been of a nervous temperament, and the effects of these combined influences is shown in the highly nervous and susceptible organisation of the orphan girls, and in a morbid sympathy of constitution, by which each appeared to suffer from any ailment of the other. This remarkable sympathy is very clearly shown in more than one of the letters I have submitted for your consideration, and I have numerous others in my possession which, should they be considered insufficient, will place the matter, irregular as it certainly is, beyond the reach of doubt. I must request you to bear it particularly and constantly in mind throughout the case.

Almost from the time of the mother's death, the children were placed in the care of a poor, but respectable woman, at Hastings. Here the younger, whose constitution appears to have been originally much stronger than that of her sister, seems to have improved rapidly in health, and in so doing to have mastered, in some degree, that morbid sympathy of temperament of which I have spoken, and which in the weaker organisation of the elder sister, still maintained its former ascendency. They were about six years old when, whether through the carelessness of the nurse or not is immaterial to us now, the younger was lost during a pleasure-excursion in the neighbourhood. Every enquiry was made, and it appeared pretty clear that she had fallen into the hands of a gang of gipsies, who at that time infested the country round; but no further trace of her was ever after discovered.

The elder sister, now left alone, seems to have been watched with redoubled solicitude. There is nothing, however, in the years immediately following Miss C. Boleton's disappearance having any direct bearing upon our case, and I have, therefore, confined my extracts from the correspondence entrusted to me, to two or three letters from a lady in whose charge she was placed at Hampstead, and one from an old friend of her mother, from which we gather the fact of her marriage. The latter is chiefly notable as pointing out the nervous and highly sensitive temperament of the young lady's husband, the late Mr. Anderton, to which I shall have occasion, at a later period of the case, more particularly to direct your attention. The former give evidence of a very important fact; namely, that of the liability of Miss Boleton to attacks of illness equally unaccountable and unmanageable, bearing a perfect resemblance to those from which she suffered in her younger days sympathetically with the ailments of her sister; and, therefore, to be not improbably attributed to a similar cause.

Thus far for the preliminary portion of the evidence. The second division places before us certain peculiarities in the

II. married life of Mrs. Anderton; its more especial object, however, being to elucidate the connection between the parties whose history we have hitherto been tracing, and the Baron R**, with whose proceedings we are properly concerned.

It appears, then, that in all respects but one, the married life of Mr. and Mrs. Anderton was particularly happy. Notwithstanding their retired and often somewhat nomad life, and the limits necessarily imposed thereby to the formation of friendships, the evidence of their devoted attachment to each other is perfectly overwhelming. I have no less than thirty-seven letters from various quarters, all speaking more or less strongly upon this point, but I have thought it better to select from the mass a small but sufficient number, than to overload the case with unnecessary repetition. In one respect alone their happiness was incomplete. It was, as had been justly observed by Mrs. Ward, most unfortunate that the choice of Miss Boleton should have fallen upon a gentleman, who, however eligible in every other respect, was, from his extreme constitutional nervousness, so peculiarly ill-adapted for union with a lady of such very similar organisation. The connection seems to have borne its natural fruit in the increased delicacy of both parties, their married life being spent in an almost continual search after health. Among the numerous experiments tried with this object, they at length appear to have had recourse to mesmerism, becoming finally patients of Baron R**, a well known professor of that and other kindred impositions.

Mrs. Anderton had not been long under his care, when the remonstrances of several friends led to the cessation of the Baron's immediate manipulations, the 'mesmeric fluid' being now conveyed to the patient through the intervention of a third party. Mademoiselle Rosalie, 'the medium' thus employed, was a young person regularly retained by Baron R** for that purpose, and of her it is necessary here to say a few words.

She appears to have been about the age of Mrs. Anderton, though looking perhaps a little older than her years; slight in figure, with dark hair and eyes, and in all respects but one answering precisely to the description of that lady's lost sister. The single difference alluded to, that of wide and clumsy feet, is amply accounted for by the nature of her former avocation. She had been for several years a tight-rope dancer, &c., in the employ of a travelling-circus proprietor; who, by his own account, had purchased her for a trifling sum of a gang of gipsies at Lewes, just at the very time when the younger Miss Boleton was stolen at Hastings by a gang whose course was tracked through Lewes to the westward. Of him she was again purchased by the Baron, who appears, even at the onset, to have exercised a singular power over her, the fascination of his glance, falling on her whilst engaged upon the stage, having compelled her to stop short in the performance of her part. There can, I think, be little doubt that this girl Rosalie was in fact the lost sister of Mrs. Anderton, and of this we shall find that the Baron R** very shortly became cognisant.

It does not appear that on the first meeting of the sisters he had any idea of the

relationship between them. He was, indeed,
perfectly ignorant of the early history of
both. The extraordinary sympathy, therefore, which immediately manifested itself
between them was not improbably set down
by him as a mere result of the 'mesmeric
rapport,' and it was not till he had been for
some weeks in attendance on Mrs. Anderton that accident led him to divine its true
origin. Nor, on the other hand, does this
singular sympathy—a sympathy manifested
in a precisely similar manner to that known
to have existed years ago between the sisters
—appear to have raised any suspicion of
the truth in the mind of either Mrs. Anderton or her husband. From the former, indeed, all mention of her early life had been
carefully kept till she had probably almost,
if not entirely, forgotten the event; while
the latter merely remembered it as a tale
which had long since ceased to possess any
present interest.

The two sisters were thus for several
weeks in the closest contact, the effects of
which may or may not have been heightened

by the so-called mesmeric connection between them, before any suspicion of their
relationship crossed the mind of anyone.
One evening, however,—and from certain
peculiar circumstances we are enabled to fix
the date precisely to the 13th of October,
1854,—the Baron appears beyond all doubt
to have become cognisant of the fact. I
must request your particular attention to
the circumstances by which his discovery of
it was attended.

On that evening the conversation appears
to have very naturally turned upon a certain extraordinary case professed to be re-
ported in a number of the ' Zoïst Mesmeric
Magazine,' published a few days before.
The pretended case was that of a lady suffering from some internal disorder which
forbade her to swallow any food, and re-
ceiving sustenance through mesmeric sympathy with the operator, who '*ate for her.*'
From this extraordinary tale the conversation turned naturally to other manifestations
of constitutional sympathy, as an instance
of which Mr. Anderton related the story of

Mrs. Anderton's lost sister, and the singular bond which had existed between them. The

II., 2. conversation appears to have continued some time, and in the course of it a jesting remark was made by one of the party in allusion to the story of eating by deputy, to which I am inclined to look as the key-note of this horrible affair.

'I said,' deposes Mr. Morton, 'I said *it was lucky for the young woman that the fellow didn't eat anything unwholesome.*'

From the moment these words were spoken the Baron appears to have dropped out of the conversation altogether. More than this, he was clearly in a condition of great mental pre-occupation and disturbance. Mr. Morton goes on to describe the singularity of his manner, the letting his cigar expire between his teeth, and the tremulousness of his hands, so excessive, that in attempting to re-light it he only succeeded in destroying that of his friend. There can, I think, be no doubt whatever that from that moment he believed thoroughly in the identity of Rosalie with the lost sister of Mrs. Anderton. What other ideas the conversation had suggested to him we must endeavour to ascertain from the evidence that follows.

On the morning of the day succeeding that on the evening of which he had become convinced of Rosalie's identity, we find Baron R** at Doctors' Commons II., 5 enquiring into the particulars of a will by which the sum of 25,000*l.* had been bequeathed, under certain conditions, to the children of Lady Boleton. Under the provisions of this will, the girl Rosalie was, after her sister and Mr. Anderton, the heir to this legacy. We need, I think, have no difficulty in connecting the acquisition of this intelligence with the steps by which it was immediately followed. Mr. Anderton at once received an intimation of the Baron's approaching departure for the continent, and at the end of the third week from that time leave was taken, and he apparently started upon his journey. In point of fact, however, his plans were of a very different character. During the three weeks which intervened between his visit to Doctors' Commons and his farewell to Mr. Anderton, there had been advertised in the parish church of Kensington the banns of marriage between himself and his 'medium,' Rosalie,—not, indeed, in the names by which they were ordinarily known, and which would very probably have excited attention, but in the family name—if so it be—of the Baron, and in that by which Rosalie was originally known when with the travelling-circus. By what means he prevailed upon his victim to consent to such a step is not important to the matter in hand. The general tenour of the subsequent evidence shows clearly that it must have been under some form of compulsion, and, indeed, the unfortunate girl seems to have been made by some means altogether subservient to his will.

The marriage thus secretly effected, the Baron and his wife leave town, not for the continent, as stated to Mr. Anderton, but for Bognor,—an out-of-the-way little watering-place on the Sussex coast, deserted save for the week of the Goodwood races,—where, at that time of the year, he was not likely to meet with any one to whom he was known. Before endeavouring to investigate the motive of all this mystery, it is necessary to bear in mind one important fact:—

Between the wife of Baron R** and Mr. Wilson's legacy of 25,000*l., the lives of Mr. and Mrs. Anderton alone intervened.*

The first few days of the Baron's stay in Bognor seem to have been devoted to the search for a servant, he having insisted on the unusual arrangement of himself providing one in the house where he lodged. It is worthy of note that the one finally selected was in a position, with respect to character, that placed her entirely in her master's power. It is unfortunate that this same defect of character necessarily lessens the value of evidence from such a source. We must, however, take it for what it is worth, remembering at the same time, that there is a total absence of any apparent motive, save that of telling the truth, for the statement she has made.

S

It appears, then, from her account, that after trying by every means to tempt her into some repetition of her former error, the Baron at last seized upon the pretext of her taking from the breakfast-table a single taste of jam upon her finger, to threaten her with immediate and utter ruin. One only loop-hole was left by which she could escape. The alternative was, indeed, most ingeniously and delicately veiled under the pretext of seeking a plausible reason for her dismissal; but, in point of fact, it amounted to this, that, as a condition of her alleged offence not being recorded against her, she would own to the commission of another with which she had nothing whatever to do.

The offence to which she was falsely to plead guilty was this: on the night succeeding the commission of the fault of which, such as it was, she was really guilty, Madame R** was taken suddenly ill. The symptoms were those of antimonial poisoning. The presence of antimony in the stomach was clearly shown. In the presence of the medical man who had been

called in, the girl was taxed by the Baron
with having administered, by way of a trick,
a dose of tartar-emetic; and she, in obedience to a strong hint from her master, con-
fessed to the delinquency, and was there-
upon dismissed with a good character in
other respects.   Freed from the dread of
exposure, she now flatly denies the whole
affair, both of the trick and of the quarrel
which was supposed to have led to it, and
I am bound to say, that looking both to ex-
ternal and internal evidence, her statement
seems worthy of credit.

Nevertheless, the poison was unquestion-
ably administered.   By whom?

Cui bono?   Certainly, it will be said, not
for that of the Baron; for until at least the
death of Mr. and Mrs. Anderton his interest
was clearly in the life of his wife.   It is not,
therefore, by any means to be supposed
that he would before that event attempt to
poison her.   Of this mystery, then, it appears that we must seek the solution elsewhere.

Returning, then, for a time to Mr. and

Mrs. Anderton, we find that the latter has
also suffered from an attack of illness.
Comparing her journal and the evidence of
her doctor, with that given in the case of
Madame R**, it appears that the
III. symptoms were identical in every
respect, with this single but important exception, that in this case there is no
apparent cause for the attack, nor can any
trace of poison be found. A little further
enquiry, and we arrive at a yet more mysterious coincidence.

It is a matter of universal experience, that
almost the most fatal enemy of crime is
over-precaution. In this particular case the
precautions of the Baron R** appear to have
been dictated by a skill and fore-thought
almost superhuman, and so admirably have
they been taken, that, save in the concealment of the marriage, it is almost impossible to recognise in them any sinister
motive whatever. His course with respect
to the servant-girl, though dictated, as we
believe, by the most criminal designs, is
perfectly consistent with motives of the

very highest philanthropy. Even in the concealment of the marriage, once granting —as I think may very fairly be granted— that such a marriage might be concealed without any necessary imputation of evil, the means adopted were equally simple, effective, and unblameable. They consisted merely in the use of the real, instead of the stage names of the contracting parties, and in the very proper avoidance of all ground for scandal by hiring another lodging, in order that before marriage the address of both parties might not be the same. In the illness of Madame R**, too, at Bognor, nothing can, to all appearance, be more straightforward than the Baron's conduct. He at once proclaims his suspicion of poison, sends for an eminent physician, verifies his doubts, administers the proper remedies, and dismisses the servant by whose fault the attack has been occasioned. Viewed with an eye of suspicion, there is indeed something questionable in the selection of the medical attendant. Why should the Baron refuse to send for either of the local

practitioners, both gentlemen of skill and reputation, and insist on calling in a stranger
to the place, who in a very few days would
leave it, and very probably return no more?
Distrust of country doctors, and decided
preference for London skill, furnishes us, as
usual, with a prompt and plausible reply. It
does not, however, exclude the possibility
that the expediency of removing as far as
possible all evidence of what had passed
may have in some degree affected the choice.
Be that as it may, this precaution, whether
originally for good or for evil, has enabled
us to fix with certainty a very important
point.

*Mrs. Anderton was taken ill, not only with
the same symptoms, but at the same time, with
Madame R**.*

Before proceeding to consider the events
which followed, there are one or two points
in the history of this first illness of the
sisters on which it is needful to remark.
The action of those metallic poisons among
which we may undoubtedly rank antimony,

is as yet but very little understood. We
know, however, from the statements of Professor Taylor,* certainly by far the first
English authority upon the subject, that
peculiarities of constitution, or, as they are
termed, 'idiosyncracies,' frequently assist
or impede to a very extraordinary extent
the action of such drugs. The constitution
of Madame R** appears to have been thus
idiosyncratically disposed to favour the action of antimony. There can be no doubt
that the action of the poison upon her system was very greatly in excess of that
which, under ordinary circumstances, would
have been expected from a similar dose.
The poison, therefore, by whomsoever administered, *was not intended to prove fatal*,
though from the peculiar idiosyncracy of
Madame R** it was very nearly doing so.

The narrowness of Madame R**'s escape
seems to have struck the Baron, and to
have exercised a strong influence over his
future proceedings. Whether or not he
knew or believed her to be exposed to any

* 'Taylor on Poisons.'   2nd edition, p. 98, et inf.

peculiar influences which might tend to render her life less secure than that of her delicate and invalid sister, it is impossible positively to say. There was no question, however, that her death before that of Mrs. Anderton would destroy all prospect of his succession to the 25,000*l.*, and with this view he proceeded to take as speedily as possible the necessary steps to secure himself against such an event. The obvious course, and indeed that suggested at once by Dr. Jones, was that of assurance, and this course he accordingly adopted, after having previously, by a tour of several months, restored his wife to a state of health in which her life would probably be accepted by the offices concerned. The insurances, therefore, with which we are concerned, were effected in consequence of a previous administration of poison to Madame R**, producing an illness far more serious than could have been anticipated, and accompanied by precisely similar symptoms on the part of her delicate sister, Mrs. Anderton, whose death, *if preceding that of Madame R**,*

would more than double the Baron's prospect of succession.

Between him, therefore, and the sum of
either 25,000*l.* or 50,000*l.* there now intervened three lives, those of Mr. and Mrs.
Anderton, and of his own wife, Madame
R * *, and on the order in which they fell
depended the amount of his gain by their
demise.   The death of Mr. Anderton before that of Mrs. Anderton, would open
the possibility of a second marriage, from
which might arise issue, whose claim
would precede his; that of his own wife,
preceding that of either Mr. or Mrs. Anderton, would destroy altogether his own
claim to the larger sum.   It was only in
the event of Mrs. Anderton's death being
followed first by that of her husband, and
afterwards by that of her sister, that the
Baron's entire claim would be secured.

*Within one year from the time at which
matters assumed this position, these three
lives fell in, and in precisely the order in
which the Baron would most largely and
securely profit by their demise.*

We now proceed to examine the circumstances under which they fell.

Immediately on his return to England, and before apparently completing his arrangements with respect to the policies of insurance, the Baron, we find, calls upon Mr. Anderton, and by dint of minute enquiries draws from him the entire history of the attack from which Mrs. Anderton had suffered several months before. Supposing, therefore, that the information was of any practical interest, the Baron was now fully aware of the perfect similarity, both of time and symptom, between the cases of his wife and her sister. It is essential that this should be borne in mind.

He now proceeds to establish himself in lodgings in Russell Place, in a house in which, for five days and every night V. in the week, he is entirely alone.

The only other tenant is a medical man, whose visits are confined to a few hours on two days in the week, and who lives at too great a distance to be called in on any sudden emergency. Here he establishes himself upon the first and second floors, with a laboratory in a small detached room upon the basement floor, where his chemical experiments can be carried on without inconvenience to the rest of the house. It is essential that the position of this laboratory should be very clearly borne in mind, as it plays a most important part in the story which is now to follow.

In these lodgings, then, Madame R** is again taken ill with a return, though in a greatly mitigated form, of the same symptoms from which she had previously suffered at Bognor. The attack, however, though less violent in its immediate effects, is succeeded at regular intervals of about a fortnight by others of a precisely similar character. And here we arrive at what is at once the most significant, the most extraordinary, and the most questionable of the evidence we have been able to collect.

It appears, then, that upon a night

VII.

in August, a young man of the name of Aldridge, who, as a matter of special favour had been taken into the house since the arrival of the Baron, saw Madame R** leave her bedroom, and, apparently in her sleep, walk down the stairs in the dark to the lower part of the house. The room in which the Baron slept was next to her's, and on the wall of that room, projected by the night-lamp burning on the table, the young man saw what seemed to be the shadow of a man watching Madame R** as she went by. He looked again, and the shadow was gone — so rapidly that at first he could scarcely believe his eyes, and was only, after consideration, satisfied that it really had been there. He went down to the room, but the Baron was—or pretended to be—asleep. He told him what had happened to Madame R**, and he at once followed her. Aldridge watched him until he had descended the kitchen-stairs and returned, followed closely by the sleep-walker. He then went back to his room, to which

the Baron shortly afterwards came to thank
him for his warning, and to tell him that,
in some freak of slumber, Madame R**
had visited the kitchen.

So far the story is simple enough. There
is nothing extraordinary in a sick woman
of exciteable nerves taking a sudden fit of
somnambulism, and walking down even
into the kitchen of a house that was not
her own.   The Baron's conduct—in all
respects but that of the watching shadow
—was precisely that which, from a sensible
and affectionate husband, might most
naturally have been expected.   Nor is it
very difficult, even setting aside all idea of
malice, to put down the shadow portion
of the story to a mere freak of imagination
on the part of the young man who, though
'not drunk,' was nevertheless on his own
admission, 'perhaps a little excited,' and
who had been 'drinking a good deal of
beer and shandy-gaff.'   But the evidence
does not end here.

By one of those extraordinary coincidences by which the simple course of or-

dinary events so often baffles the best
laid schemes of crime, there were others
in the house besides the young man,
Aldridge, who witnessed the movements
of the Baron and Madame R**. It so
happened that, on the afternoon of that
particular day, the woman of the house
had hampered the little latch-lock by which
young Aldridge usually admitted himself,
and, as this occurred late in the day, it is
more than probable that the Baron was
unaware of it, as also of the fact that in
consequence the servant-girl, Susan Turner,
sat up beyond the usual hour of going to
bed, for the purpose of letting the young
man in. This girl, it seems, had a lover
—a stoker on one of the northern lines—
and him she appears to have invited to
keep her company on her watch. Aldridge
returned and went up to bed, but the lover
—who was to be on duty with his engine
at two o'clock, and who was doubtlessly
interrupted in a most interesting conversation by the arrival of the lodger—still
remained in the kitchen, and was only

just leaving it when Madame R** came down stairs. Taking her at first to be the mistress of the house, and fearful lest the street-lamp gleaming through the glass partition should betray her 'young man's' presence, Susan Turner draws him to the lumber-room, the window of which, it appears, looks into a sort of well between the house and the two rooms built out at the back, after a fashion not unusual in London houses. Into this well, also, immediately opposite to the window of the lumber-room, looks that of the back room or laboratory, furnished with what the witness describes as a 'tin looking-glass,' but which is really one of those metal reflectors in common use for increasing the light of rooms in such a position. The distance between the two windows is little more than eight feet. The night was clear, with a bright, full harvest moon, and its rays, thrown by the reflector into the laboratory, made every part of its interior distinctly visible from the lumber-room. The door of the latter room was open, and

the staircase illuminated by the Baron's
approaching light. The hiders in the
lumber-room could see distinctly the whole
proceedings of both Baron and Madame
R**, from the time Aldridge lost sight of
them to the moment they again emerged
into his view.

And this was what they saw:—

' *Madame R** never went into the kitchen
at all ;* ' ' *she went straight into the laboratory,*'—' *the Baron watched her as she came
out.*'

A glance at the place will show the
bearing of this evidence, and the impossibility of the Baron (who, if he had not
been in the kitchen, must at least have
thoroughly known the position of his own
laboratory) having made any mistake on
this point.

What, then, was his motive in thus im-
posing upon Aldridge, to whose interference
he professed himself so much indebted,
with this false statement of the place to
which Madame R** had been?

There does not seem the slightest reason

for discrediting the evidence of these two witnesses. Their story is perfectly simple and coherent. There is neither malice against the Baron nor collusion with Aldridge, in whose case such malice is supposed to exist. The only weak point in their position is the fact, that they were both doing wrong in being in that place at that time; but the admission of this, in truth, rather strengthens than injures the testimony which involves it. We must seek the clue, then, not in their motives, but in those of the Baron. The errand of Madame R**, in her strange expedition, may perhaps afford it. What did she do in the laboratory?

' She drank something from a bottle.' *' It smelt and tasted like sherry.'* *' It was marked* VIN. ANT. POT. TART.*' That label designates antimonial wine, which is a mixture of sherry and tartar-emetic.*

Let us see if from this point we can feel our way, as it were, backwards, to the motive for concealment. The life of Madame R** was, as we know, heavily in-

sured. It had already been seriously
endangered by the effects of precisely the
same drug as that she was now seen to
take. If the Baron knew or suspected
the motive of her visit, here is at once a
motive sufficient, if not perhaps very credit-
able, for the concealment of a fact, the
knowledge of which might very probably
lead to difficulty with respect to payment
of the policy in case of death.

But here another difficulty meets us.
The incident in question occurred at about
the middle of the long illness of Madame
R**. That illness consisted of a series of
attacks, occurring as nearly as possible at
intervals of a fortnight, and exhibiting the
exact symptoms of the poison here shown
to have been taken. One of the attacks
followed within a very few hours of the
occurrence into which we are examining.
Was it the only occurrence of the kind?

The evidence of the night-nurse bears
with terrible weight upon this point. Her
orders are strict, on no account to close
her eyes. Her hours of watch are short,

and the repose of the entire day leaves her
without the slightest cause for unusual
drowsiness.   The testimonials of twenty
years bear unvarying witness to her care
and trustworthiness.   Yet every alternate
Saturday for eight or ten, or it may even
have been twelve weeks, at one regular
hour she falls asleep.   It is in vain that
she watches and fights against it—in vain
even that, suspecting 'some trick' she on
one occasion abstains entirely from food,
and drinks nothing but that peculiarly
wakeful decoction, strong green tea.   On
every other night she keeps awake with
ease, but surely as the fatal Saturday
comes round she again succumbs, and
surely as sleep steals over her it is followed by a fresh attack of the symptoms
we so plainly recognise.   She cannot in
any way account for such an extraordinary
fatality.   She is positive that such a thing
never happened to her before.   We also
are at an equal loss.   We can but pause
upon the reflection that twice before the
periodic drowsiness began, a similarly irre-

sistible sleep had been induced by the so-called mesmeric powers of the Baron himself. And then we pass naturally to her who had been for years habituated to such control, and we cannot but call to mind the statement of Mr. Hands—' I have often *willed* her (S. Parsons) to go into a dark room and pick up a pin, or some article equally minute.'

And then we again remember the watching shadow on the wall.

And yet, after all, at what have we arrived? Grant that the Baron knew the nature of his wife's errand in the laboratory; that the singular power — call it what we will—by which he had before in jest compelled the nurse to sleep, was really employed in enabling the somnambulist to elude her watch. Grant even that the pretensions of the mesmerist are true, and that it was in obedience to his direct will that Madame R** acted as she did, we are no nearer a solution than before.

It was not the Baron's interest that his wife should die.

We must then seek further afield for any explanation of this terrible enigma. Let us see how it fared with Mrs. Anderton while these events were passing at her sister's house.

And here we seem to have another instance of the manner in which the wisest precautions so often turn against those by whom they are taken. Admitting that the illness of Madame R** was really caused by criminal means, nothing could be wiser than the precaution which selected for their first essay a night on which they could be tried without fear of observation. Yet this very circumstance enables us to fix a date of the last importance, which without it must have remained uncertain. Madame R**, then, was taken ill on Saturday, the 5th of April. On that very night—at, as nearly as can be ascertained, the very same hour, Mrs. Anderton was unaccountably seized with an illness in all respects resem-

III. and V.

bling her's. Like her's, too, the attacks returned at fortnightly intervals. For a few days, on the Baron's advice, a particular medicine is given, and at first with apparently good effect. At the same date the diary of Dr. Marsden shows a similar amelioration of symptoms in the case of Madame R**. In both cases the amendment is but short, and the disease again pursues its course. The result in both is utter exhaustion. In the case of Madame R** reducing the sufferer to death's door; in the *weaker constitution* of her sister terminating in death. Examination is made. The appearances of the body, no less than the symptoms exhibited in life, are all those of antimonial poisoning. No antimony is, however, found; and from this, and other circumstances, results a verdict of ' Natural Death.' On the 12th of October, then, Mrs. Anderton's story ends.

*From that time dates the recovery of Madame R**.*

The first life is now removed from be-

tween Baron R** and the full sum of
50,000*l*. Let us examine briefly the circumstances attending the lapse of
the second.   Here again events each VI.
in itself quite simple and natural,
combine to form a story fraught with terrible suspicion.   I have alluded to the
inquest which followed on the death of Mrs.
Anderton.   That enquiry originated in
circumstances which cast upon her husband
the entire suspicion of her murder.   To
whose agency,—whether direct or indirect,
voluntary or involuntary, is an after question,—may every one of these circumstances
be traced? Mr. Anderton insists on being
the only one from whom the patient shall
receive either medicine or food.   It is the
Baron who applauds and encourages a line
of conduct *diametrically opposed to his
own*, and tending more than any other circumstance to fix suspicion on his friend. A
remedy is suggested, the recommending of
which points strongly to the idea of poison,
and it is from the Baron that the sugges-
tions comes.   Two papers are found—the

one bearing in part, the other in full,
the name of the poison suspected to be
used.　The first of these is brought to
light by the Baron himself,—the second is
found in a place where he has just been,
and by a person whom he has himself despatched to search there for something else.
He draws continual attention to that point
of exclusive attendance from which suspicion chiefly springs.　His replies to Dr.
Dodsworth, respecting the recommendation
of the antimonial antidote, are so given as
to confirm the worst interpretation to which
it had given rise, and even when, on the
discovery of the second paper, he advises
the nurse that it should be destroyed, he
does so in a manner that ensures not only
its preservation but its immediate employment in the manner most dangerous to his
friend.

The evidence fails.　What is the Baron's
connection with the catastrophe that follows?　He knows well the accused man's
nervous anxiety for his own good name.
He procures, on the ground of his friendly

anxiety, the earliest intelligence of his friend's probable acquittal.   He enters that friend's room to acquaint him with the good news.   Returning, he takes measures to secure the prisoner throughout the night from interruption or interference.   In the morning Mr. Anderton is a corpse, and on his pillow is found the phial in which the poison had been contained, and a written statement that the desperate step had been taken in despair of an acquittal.   By what marvellous accident was the hopeful news of the chemical investigation thus misinterpreted?   By what negligence or connivance was the fatal drug placed within his reach?   One thing only we know:—

It was the Baron who conveyed the news. It was from his pocket medicine-case, left by him within the sick man's reach, that the poison came.

Thus fell the second of the two lives which stood between the Baron and the full sum of 50,000*l.*   Of this sum, the 25,000*l.* which accrues from the relation-

ship between Mrs. Anderton and Madame
R** is already his as soon as claimed, but
there is no immediate necessity for the claim
to be preferred.   He may perhaps have
thought it better to wait before making
such a claim until the first sensation occasioned by the double deaths through which
he inherited had passed away.   He may
have been merely putting in train some
plausible story to account for his only now
proclaiming a fact of which he had certainly
been aware for at least a year.   Whatever
his reason, however, he certainly for some
weeks after Mr. Anderton's death made no
movement to establish his claim upon the
property, and during this time Madame
R** was slowly but surely recovering her
strength.

But while wisdom thus dictated a policy
of delay, the irresistible course of events
VII. hurried on the crisis. A letter comes
filled with threats of the vengeance
of jealous love, if its cause be not
that night removed.   It is but a fragment
of that letter that is preserved, but its

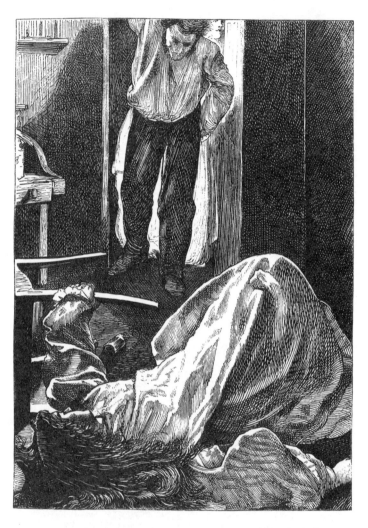

One shrill and quickly stifled shriek alarms the inmates of the house, and when they hurry to the spot they find only a disfigured corpse, lying with bare feet and disordered night dress in the darkness of the stormy November night, and with the fatal glass still clasped in its hand.